Honey Girl

Lisa Freeman

Sky Pony Press
New York

Sky Pony Press books may be purchased in bulk at special discounts for sales promotion, corporate gifts, fund-raising, or educational purposes. Special editions can also be created to specifications. For details, contact the Special Sales Department, Sky Pony Press, 307 West 36th Street, 11th Floor, New York, NY 10018 or info@skyhorsepublishing.com.

Sky Pony® is a registered trademark of Skyhorse Publishing, Inc.®, a Delaware corporation.

Visit our website at www.skyponypress.com.

10 9 8 7 6 5 4 3 2 1

Library of Congress Cataloging-in-Publication Data is available on file.

Cover design by Sarah Brody
Cover photo credit: Shutterstock

A portion of all proceeds from this novel go to the Hawaii Community Foundation to help Hawaiian artists achieve their dreams.

Print ISBN: 978-1-63220-425-7
Ebook ISBN: 978-1-63220-908-5

Printed in the United States of America

For
Phranc

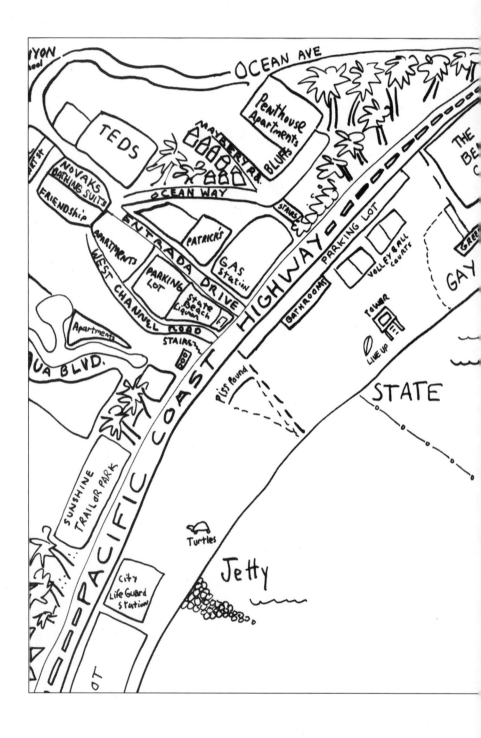

CONTENTS

I

lune

June 18–30, 1972

Cancer

CHAPTER ONE

Rulers of the World

My sickest secret is about Dad. I stole his ashes and filled his internment box with sand, ground-up puka shells, and a mashed-up plastic necklace from a vintage shop in the Hawaiian Village. I gave it to my mom with the fake remains after she came back from the mainland with Uncle Mike. The freakiest part of the whole thing is that she sleeps with the box next to her bed. She thinks that someday her ashes and Dad's will be buried together. Sorry about that. I loved my dad more than any other person on the planet. I just didn't think about what the long-term karma would be.

Here's the thing: Hawaiian men like my dad don't get buried. They get a paddle out. I knew exactly how Dad would have wanted his memorial to be. He'd have all his pals sitting on their boards in the water and family in canoes. We'd form a big circle and we'd sing songs and throw leis while his ashes were scattered in the ocean, the place he loved most. Simple. But my mom went Catholic after Dad's heart attack. She got priests and an undertaker and a crypt. She put Dad on display after someone dressed him in a suit he didn't own, combed his hair to the wrong side, and put make up on him so he didn't look so dead. She even put a wooden cross in his hands. My dad hated all that Jesus voodoo. I wasn't surprised when no one on Oahu came to the mortuary.

Mom and I sat there along with Uncle Mike and his new girlfriend, watching little gnats buzz around Dad's nostrils as the day heated up. We listened to Alfred Apaka albums while Uncle Mike made small talk.

Thank God my mom decided to finally cremate him and ditch the whole grave thing. My plan was to give Dad a secret paddle out. I collected Dad from the mortuary, brought him home, switched the ashes, and put him in a shoebox. I was on my way to the beach when Mom walked through the front door three hours early. She was all excited about the new home we'd be moving to in Santa Monica, but all I could think about was where to hide Dad.

The new plan was genius if I do say so myself. Like some cosmic pot dealer who sealed up bags of weed airtight, I poured Dad into a Ziploc baggie and made sure there were no air pockets so he wouldn't get soggy. Then I took apart my talking Mrs. Beasley doll. She was from my favorite TV show *Family Affair*. I fit Dad into her torso, stuffed him up under her voice box, and carefully distributed the ashes evenly so Mrs. Beasley wouldn't get lopsided. I was very proud of myself for pulling this off on the spur of the moment.

Everything was cool until I came home from school the next day. Mom had packed and shipped all my stuff to California, including Mrs. Beasley. I got totally tweaked out and wrapped my hair around my arm so it looked like a snake, then pulled it tight to cut off circulation. After an hour of watching my skin turn colors, I came up with a final plan that would start as soon as we got to Santa Monica.

Imagining State Beach and actually being here were two different things. Before today, I'd never been on a beach where I didn't know anyone. Dad's been gone sixty-four days. I've put some of his ashes in a Band-Aid box and, once I've got the place checked out, I'll sprinkle them in the ocean bit by bit. The box isn't big, but it's made of metal, which keeps Dad safe and dry until I let him go. When I find the right times to let him fly, I'll do a little Hawaiian ritual in my mind and remind myself that I'm standing in the Pacific Ocean. The good news is that all currents lead home to Oahu. The bad news is that with this tiny Band-Aid box, I'll probably be like twenty-five by the time Mrs. Beasley is empty.

Right now I'm almost sixteen, five-foot-six without an ounce of baby fat. I look like a model or something. No way could you tell that I used to be a kind of ugly smarty-pants kid who skipped first grade. Something happened to me when we moved. For the first time in my life, I didn't have to be that *hapa haole*, a half-half girl with my mother's hazel eyes and a lighter version of my father's brown skin. Now I would be the most Hawaiian looking person on the beach, especially with my puka shell earrings and *Waialua* mismatched bikini. It made me feel exotic and grown up. I was determined to leave behind my previous identity and create a new mystique around me.

On Sundays, hot surf spots like State are jam-packed. I had to weave around tight lines of towels slowly so as to not step on anyone's head. Naturally, there were volleyball courts. That's where guys too old to surf sat in faded blue canvas chairs, smoking Pall Malls, joking about Nixon's reelection campaign and how George McGovern didn't have a chance. You see, I'm a supernova Virgo. That means I'm observant and good at figuring stuff out. Nothing gets past me.

State was not like the beaches back home, but it did have some cool four- to six-footers. There were lots of guys on boards waiting for the next set, but I knew better than to look at them. If the local girls saw me as a predator moving in on their boyfriends, I'd be eaten alive. That meant I'd also be alone, and there's nothing worse in the world than to be alone. I had to get right with State or else it would be just me and my mom—and that would be totally terrible.

I could see the surfers in the take-off zone watching me. I kept walking. I had to be careful not to look like I was rushing or stopping. *Look normal,* I told myself. My pulse pounded in my head. All I could really focus on was left foot first and then right. That's when I saw them.

The coolest girls sat like goddesses at the shoreline. There were eight of them perched on a mound of sand that separated them from everyone else. No one dared sit in front of them or block their view of the waves, their boyfriends, or anything else they were scoping out. They were perfect in their titty-fantastic bikinis with spaghetti strap ties and low-cut legs. Looking at them made me dizzy. They were total foxes. I'd never seen so many blondes with long hair before. I wanted to scream and swim home to Oahu. I could barely breathe.

The only way I could keep walking was to imagine the lineup as cookies cooling on a rack. Some were baked brown with crispy edges. Others were topped with a crystallized glaze. They all were enticing, but in the middle of the lineup were two beastly beautiful creatures. The ultra-blonde looked like a lemon verbena cookie, bittersweet with a marshmallow center. The brunette with sun-soaked highlights next to her had huge buttercream breasts. Her hair was the color of macadamia nuts mixed with brown sugar and orange peels. She looked smooth and easy to roll, the kind of cookie that spreads out when you bake it. Miss Macadamia was blended with enough flour to have skin like mine, but what really scored was her mean peppermint smirk, which melted away when she saw me. It looked like she got socked in the stomach. I turned around to see if someone was behind me. No one was there except a bunch of hippie girls sewing patches on their jeans.

I stood still. How had she spotted me walking on a crowded beach? Maybe she could smell my *hanawai* blood. There was no way I could check my tampon string. It had to be still tucked up where it belonged. At least I hoped it was.

My mother's voice sounded in my mind.

"You can only make a first impression once," she'd say.

I stood up straight. I tilted my head so the cigarette behind my ear would drop all cool and casual into the palm of my hand. I tried to keep a mellow, unfazed look on my face. I zigzagged around the maze of towels 'til I made it to the water.

A minute seemed like an hour. I had to be on guard, like a soldier in Vietnam, with the enemy all around me. My mission was to make contact and pull back. But now I was in the danger zone. My feet were in the water, surfers were in front of me, the lineup was behind me. The only way out was through the locals' turf. I had to walk right in front of the lineup, let them check me out, and split. My stomach was doing somersaults, but there was one talisman I could always count on—my hair. It fell to the right and shielded my face from the lineup. It was like a magic cloak that covered me from the top of my head to my hips. The trick was I could see out, and they couldn't see in.

One-by-one, Miss Macadamia and her crew rolled over and gave me the stink eye. I didn't expect a warm welcome. Any halfwit from Hawaii knew that an intimidating greeting was beach protocol. But what caught me off guard was how these *haole* mainland girls looked me up and down. They didn't miss anything. Especially Miss Macadamia; she was hard-core. She looked like Raquel Welch, but younger. She examined me from my peace bead anklets to shaved bikini line. I felt naked in my crocheted bathing suit top. It fit tight and opened over my skin like tiny spiderwebs; it was from the North Shore and had lots of mojo sewn into it. I knew that because Annie Iopa, the *akua wahine*, had worn it before me. Without my friend Annie, I wouldn't have made it this far. She told me, "You are a daughter of Pele—no one can mess with you as long as she breathes fire."

I dropped my Don Ho wraparound shades over my eyes. He was a famous singer in Hawaii and I knew him. These were actually his sunglasses. They were a little too big for me but that didn't matter. I felt cool.

Miss Macadamia gave a tiny nod and all her girls sat up in unison. Frowns covered their faces as they watched my feet touch their beach. It felt like I was walking on the rim of an active volcano. I had to move slowly or else they would know I was panicking. Up close, these girls could not be dismissed as cookies. Blonde hair, scarves, and barrettes aside, they were full-on "locals" just like the ones at home. Feeling their bad vibes, I quickly reviewed Annie's rules on how to deal with mainland locals.

THE RULES:
1. **Let locals get a good look at you.**
2. **Show no fear and walk slowly.**
3. **Sit off their beach but where locals can see you.**
4. **Treat everyone on a new beach with respect.**
5. **Locals make contact first. Locals rule.**

I knew that these girls were only cocky sixteen-year-olds who probably just got their braces taken off. But whether they liked me or not was a matter of life and death. Only losers like my mom end up alone. When I finally got the courage to look in their direction, they were looking at someone else. Was I dismissed? Was it over? That wasn't fair. Crimson heat streaked down my cheeks. I had to do something quick. Back home, the girls in this lineup would have been painting their noses with zinc and kissing my semi-brown ass.

They had no idea who they were screwing with. I knew girls on the island with hair so long it touched the ground and others who were so tough, *titas*, they'd kick the crap out of them just for being blonde. What could these *haoles* do to me? I've seen Gerry Lopez in person. He's the best surfer in the world, even though he's a goofy foot. And now he's a movie star, too. Just wait until these *haole* dumbos see *Five Summer Stories*. They won't know what hit them. Gerry Lopez, Mr. Pipeline, surfing twenty-footers.

I've seen bigger waves at Makaha. Of course, I was ten at the time and my dad made me sit in the car, but they didn't need to know the details. Bottom line, I knew beach craft. I was as good as or better than any of them. To prove it, I stopped right in front of them and splashed my feet. That got their attention. In the wind, I lit another cigarette and did a full hair flip before turning my back to them and blowing out the match. It was major. If I were in the Munich Olympics, I would have just gotten the gold for cool.

I took a long drag off my Lark 100 and looked up. That's when Miss Macadamia busted me. She rested a few fingers against her cheek and, without the others noticing, stuck her tongue out at me. Not like "nah-nah-nah," but pointed and curled up. She moved it real slow, like the Great Tyrant did in my favorite movie *Barbarella*. I continued walking as though nothing happened. I recorded every little detail in my mind to review later.

Miss Macadamia sat up slowly. Her silky bikini was smaller than mine and she sat cross-legged with almost everything showing. Unreal. She was beyond skewed, but I didn't react. I kept walking. Miss Macadamia stared, shredding me with invisible daggers, tearing through layers of skin. She was super pretty looking on the surface but definitely nasty inside, the perfect combo to rule a beach like State. This was way too intense. I hadn't been so freaked out since Sam Mishima showed me his mother's Ben Wa balls.

I trudged though the scalding sand. The California sun was so bright I was forced to squint even with my shades on. Then it occurred to me that I had passed their test. I had survived. In my strained peripheral vision, I could see the last and least important girl in the lineup. Why was she smiling at me? What a dork. She looked my age or maybe a little younger. I picked up my pace. I was almost at the storm drain when I heard her.

"Hey, Five-O," she shouted.

The sarcastic tone made me realize exactly who she was. She was the one with nothing to lose, the wild card in the lineup trying to prove herself. I turned because I had to. I couldn't believe someone my age could hold such a gangster stance. She was standing with one hand on her hip and the other waving a cigarette. Her long ringlets were freakish white and hung loosely down her back. She looked like Shirley Temple on acid. She stood there like a dancer in first position, but there was no way this chick was a ballerina. She was probably just a volleyball jock.

The lineup snickered. Each girl leaned forward on one elbow to watch. My legs felt like lead weights. I instantly understood how animals got run over on highways.

"Give her a light," Miss Macadamia demanded.

Her voice was soft but firm. My heart sank when the Wild Card Girl waved her cigarette around like a sword.

There was no time to lose. I had to do something. I thought about two other things my mother always told me.

"A girl can catch more flies with honey" and "When in doubt, smile."

So I smiled. I raised my shades up and forced a pleasant look onto my face. So what if they saw my weird green eyes and the space between my front teeth? I had to totally go for it.

I thought of the ladies who sold sweet corn from roadside stands in Hilo. I imitated the way they lifted their heads and looked up with their eyes. These women could squeeze kindness out of anybody by using the breath prayer. They had a *kala aloha* power: steadfast, loyal, and faithful, which mainland girls had no clue about. I didn't have it. But the killers in this lineup didn't know that. If I was really going to recreate myself, this was the perfect opportunity to introduce the new me.

I walked toward Miss Wild Card. I felt my face turn into warm glowing sunlight that filled the space between us. The girl who had been so brave and sassy stepped back. I kept moving toward her, she kept backing away. Miss Macadamia was pissed and stood up fast. She had to protect her territory. Now that she was on her feet, I could see she was a real centerfold type. Her boobs were really, really big, her waist was tiny, and her stomach was flat as a board. I tossed the book of matches in my hand over the chicken girl's head and into Miss Macadamia's hands. Naturally, she caught them easily. According to Annie's rules, now that one of them had talked to me, I could talk back.

"Keep 'em," I said in my sweetest aloha voice.

Miss Macadamia gave the matches to Miss Lemon Verbena after she lit up their smokes. Then she picked up the joint that fell out of the flying matchbook.

"Thanks," she said.

The ultra-cool local goddess had my matchbook from Kammie's on the North Shore and a killer joint of Maui Wowie from my dad's stash. This meant the lineup had their introduction and I had mine. All I had to do was wait. They'd make the next move.

CHAPTER TWO

The Law Giver

Annie Iopa didn't have a clue who the last president was or why the United States was fighting in Vietnam, but she knew how to walk softly on hot sand and sashay around dog poop without looking down. If it weren't for Annie, I never would have made it past the lineup or learned about astrology.

Just like Annie had instructed, I sat at the Jetty, the beach a few hundred feet from State where the lineup could see me. The Jetty was a longboarders break with one- to three-footers. Guys who surf longboards are usually park rangers or married men so I knew they wouldn't bother me.

I laid my towel out so that I could keep an eye on everything that was going down. So far, I'd done things perfectly and I rewarded myself with a bag of M&Ms.

Annie Iopa was like a genius when it came to surfers and local girl bureaucracy. A Capricorn and legend in her own time, she could outmaneuver anyone on the beach with her long wavy hair, killer body, and bright white smile. She was the number one hostess at Dad's bar. Before that, she was the full-on North Shore *wahine kapu*, which meant that she was powerful. Capricorns are dependable and committed to their friends. Annie made that clear in her perfect combo of strength and beauty. It got her in with all the pros, like Buffalo Keaulana and Paul Strauch. Surfers trusted Annie since she knew everything about giant waves and liked to say, "Waves sewed heaven and earth together."

Annie loved my dad, but not lovey-dovey like my mom did. In fact, Annie was the first person to visit my house when news about his heart attack hit the coconut wireless. That day and every day after, Annie's voice was as soothing as Valium to me. I loved to hear her retell stories about surfers. She could talk about them for hours. She'd say, "Surfers were messengers, priests, and gods disguised as mortal men."

Another thing she said was that "only a few of those planet-bound spirits could handle the *hana kuli* of the giant waves."

Annie was like a poet when she talked about the ocean.

"The sound of the waves that crashed and died on shallow reefs," she said, moving her long fingers in the air, "could crush eardrums with their screams."

She called them "water monsters." Sometimes, she said, the noise they made was like "a million jets taking off at the same time." Then she'd close her eyes and say, "That sound made a man pray for forgiveness."

Annie talked about surfing like it was a religion.

Real surfers treat the ocean with reverence. Annie told me about the day a jerk professional football player took on Makaha to show off to his buddies. She said he mouthed off to the locals and showed no respect for the waves. It made her laugh when he got caught in a swell and washed up on shore with coral sticking out of his cheeks. Big waves can humble even the most conceited guys real quick. The ocean is to be worshiped, not pissed in.

Dad took me to see the big waves lots of times. Mom would go nuts because the highway always got washed out and it was so dangerous, but it was one of our special times together so we went anyway. Dad would say, "Your cute mommy got lots of worries."

I shifted my towel to face the sun. In the distance, I studied the lineup of girls hanging out with some hunks. The no surf flag—yellow with a black ball in the center—was up, which explained why the guys were out of the water. The late afternoon wind was making all these white caps and the ocean looked angry and cold. I concentrated on Annie, closed my eyes, and remembered how beautiful she was with black hair to her knees.

I could see her clearly in my mind. I have a photographic memory; I remember images as if they were snapshots. Annie told me that there's magic in that. She said it was a gift that I could make real whatever I imagined. All I had to do was picture something over and over and it would come true sooner or later. I was an extra powerful Virgo born under a special star. Annie called me a supernova Virgo. That's why she turned me onto astrology. The stars, she said, would guide me. Really, it was Linda Goodman's book, *Sun Signs*, and Sydney Omarr's daily horoscope column in the paper that explained how it worked. I could create a new reality.

No one would ever know about my special skill or how I used the sky to understand who and what mattered.

This is how it works: I close my eyes and enter a dream chamber in my mind. It's where I go to figure things out. These days it's purple and sparkly, nothing like the Chamber of Dreams in the movie *Barbarella* that gave me the idea in the first place. I imagine people I want to know as specific signs. Once I have a person identified as a Libra or something, it's easy to weave a path in or out of his or her life.

After Dad died, Annie gave me her lucky blue rabbit foot. I had lots of stinky thoughts at that time and she promised it would protect me. All I had to do was think positively and rub it. But when it came to life on a new beach, she said I had to remember every rule and regulation she taught me. That would be the difference between me getting in or getting lost at State. Annie had seen my potential. She had been grooming me to take her place up north someday. No way was I going to let all our work go to waste.

"Think of the mainland as a *Wahine* School," Annie told me.

And that's exactly what I was doing.

CHAPTER THREE

Credo

The next few days, I got to the Jetty around 10:30 in the morning. I made sure to enter from the California Incline side even though it was a longer walk. What I liked about the hike was seeing the statue of Saint Monica at the end of Wilshire Boulevard because it looked like a giant hard-on I'd seen in a dirty magazine. In the morning, maids who worked at the Miramar Hotel across the street would leave flowers at her feet. The red geraniums looked good in my hair.

It wasn't safe for non-locals to enter through State's tunnels that weaved under the Pacific Coast Highway, a.k.a. PCH, or to park in its public lot. No one hangs unless they're invited. Annie told me that was the universal surf law of locals and of course she was right. The locals had sentinels watching from the bluffs above and three nasty generals keeping a lookout on the ground. There was no way I would ever try the main entrance unless the lineup gave me a thumbs up.

Only one person could move around State wherever he wanted. Every beach had one: a bum who dug through the trash and slept in the sand. In Hawaii, we called them *kanaka pupule*, but I nicknamed State Beach's bum *Lōlō*. Which is pidgin for crazy. Back home, pidgin is day-to-day local talk, kind of a mix of Creole, English, and Hawaiian. All day Lōlō walked back and forth across the beach and around the parking lot and the liquor store talking to himself. He leaned on a tall driftwood stick and wore a wool Salvation Army blanket over his shoulders like a cape. He had a beard and hair sprouted out of the top of his head like a cornfield and, like most bums, he had a dog.

Beach dogs were shelter freaks or highway rescues. What was spooky about Lōlō's dog was that it sensed me watching him. Even from a distance, I could tell the dog didn't like me. I'd see him rotate his ears back and turn in my direction. He creeped me out. I wanted to stay far away from that hound. He crinkled his long muzzle and sniffed, then raised his big, egg-shaped head real slow. I'd never seen a dog like him before. He was muscular and stocky, low to the sand with eyes that were really far apart, black and narrow. That dog looked like something from another planet.

I lay in the sun watching Lōlō. An astrological sign formed in my mind. It was the first one that connected me to State Beach. I knew I was looking at more than a dog and a bum who pulled moldy bread from the trash. There was something mystical going on with them. The sign that came to me was about being alone but being okay. It was about traveling with patience. It told me I had to trust my instincts and wait for a guide. Lōlō must have been a Sagittarius. Yeah, that explained it.

The beach was quiet during the week. There was no one at the Jetty except a regular group of old gals who called themselves The Turtles. They swam three times a day and ate tuna fish sandwiches that stunk up the place. Although they were locals, they didn't seem to mind me sitting in the same spot every morning just to their left.

I'd never sat alone on a beach before. It was the first time I noticed how big the ocean really was. The Turtles were my only comfort along with Dad's thermos filled with what had been his morning protein drink. Even though he was gone, I still made it every day. I carefully unscrewed the top and took several long breaths. The smell of it made me feel safe and cozy.

In Hawaii, the drink is called Hair of the Dolphin. I called it a Daddy-tini. It was a mixture of protein powder, wheat germ, ginseng, bee pollen, one cup orange juice, and one cup vodka. Every morning I'd make it for my dad. Put it in a blender sometimes with fruit if there was papaya or mango in the freezer. Sometimes he even added lychee juice or coconut and ginger.

I knew everything about bars and being a bartender. I knew the exact amount of a dash, jigger, scoop, split, and pony. Bartenders had rules, too. The most important was: always measure exactly and put the ingredients in order. That made all the difference in the world. I knew how to cut citrus peels, stack swizzle sticks, tell the difference between a shot glass and a hurricane glass, make a hot toddy or Tropicana, and shake up a Zoom like a milk shake with honey, ice cream, and eggs. I knew a virgin had no alcohol in it, Sloe

Gin Fizzes got their red color from the berries on blackthorn bushes, sangria was punch soda, wine, and juice, and a Puff had milk and alcohol in it. And I knew you should never skimp on ice when making a cocktail.

My dad's bar, the Java Jones, was known for its drinks with a kick. He was a bartender who liked to see people having a good time, but his rule was: never drink at the office. That's why I did his morning pick-me-up special at home. Sometimes I'd even make them before I went to school so he'd have it when he woke up. Now I just make them to remind me of him.

I put the lid back on and screwed it tight, placing it safely in my purse until I needed to smell it again.

I had to organize my thoughts. Thinking about my dad made me want to cry. To refocus, all I had to do was think of Annie. She always shaved her kneecaps and oiled them in cocoa butter so they wouldn't peel. She did the same with her elbows, feet, and palms. It gave her a sparkle that lasted all day. She showed me how to get rid of deodorant streaks under my arms with a Q-tip and clip split ends with nail scissors. We used to wash our hair together and rinse it with vinegar before going to the beach to make it shine. She showed me how to pick up a towel without flicking sand, flip my hair in the wind, and light up on the first try.

Lighting up, like every beach stance, was a hula. No movements were trivial. Everything meant something. Annie taught me how to sneeze without opening my mouth and look up without lifting my head. In the water, she told me to think like a girl and swim like a shark.

"Show no mercy," she always said. She was always reminding me that on a locals-only beach survival was the only goal.

She also taught me how to make my weird eyes do all the talking. One thing I want to make clear is that my eyes aren't crossed or anything. The big problem with my eyes is they stand out. What makes them weird is the color. They're deep set and really light brown with yellow in the middle. My mother calls them hazel. I call them green. They are the first thing people notice about me.

There were two other important rules Annie told me about. They were:

Never enter the water when surfers are out.
And never ever surf under any circumstances.

"Girls don't surf," Annie said.

The first time she told me that, I thought it was odd. What about Mo'o the Lizard Goddess, who snagged a lover when she was surfing? What about Kelea, the great woman chief who was surfing when she got kidnapped? And what about Margo Oberg, the blonde girl who surfs Makaha?

Then Annie told me what happened to girls who surfed. It was awful. First, guys would label them losers or dykes and that was the worst thing in the world. But the main thing was girls hated girls who surfed. They thought of them as troublemakers who were messing with the natural flow of a beach. Once that happened, no one would ever go near them again. Even if a girl was getting gang banged, locals would stay clear. Annie told me she'd seen it happen but couldn't do anything. It was another rule:

Never interfere with surf politics.

The cool thing about all this stuff Annie taught me was that surfers had no idea The Rules existed. It was a girl manifesto, unnamed and coded, passed down from generation to generation.

"We are like the air," Annie told me. "We are everywhere, yet no one sees us."

I understood what Annie meant, but that's not exactly how it works. You see, we aren't invisible, as a matter of fact, we're far from it. We're the type of girls who don't have to look both ways to cross the street; we know the traffic will stop. Our style of long hair and flowing clothes make us look like we are floating. Each one of us creates our own look—and someday I will, too.

The term used to describe Annie and the kind of local I want to be is Honey Girl. That's what guys in Hawaii call the super sweet, nice girls. Surfers, on the other hand, use the word a bit differently. The story goes: there was once a big-time surfer at Waimea who came out of the water totally dazed. Everyone thought he got hit in the head by his board until he pointed to a major *wahine*. She was so dreamy and sexy pretty, there wasn't a word to describe her until he spit out, "Honey Girl."

If I'm lucky, I will become the first official combo sexy-sweet Honey Girl at State Beach. That is, if I get in with the lineup.

Like I said, we have a totally underground society, a secret girl world that surfers really know nothing about even though it's right in front of them. Girls rule girls on the beach. Girls have the power to mentor or destroy each other. That meant that for me to get local status, Miss Macadamia and Lemon Verbena would have to take me in. There was no other way. I would have to be their protégée. Lemon Verbena and Macadamia would decide my fate. They would give me my beach pass or keep it from me. If I got lucky, they'd train me to rule the beach before they turned eighteen and left.

Annie told me the law about leaving the beach was never mentioned. But the truth was all "girl rulers" had to leave the beach on their eighteenth birthday or they'd lose status. Oh, sure, a ruler could return to her beach but she could never stay all day every day like she used to. If she did, she'd look like a flash in the pan with nowhere to go. Annie said that a real local goddess dies when she graduates high school and morphs into something better.

I closed my eyes tight and went into my dream chamber. I saw those two beasts as my best friends, just loving me up. They had to. I was almost sixteen and time was tight. My life would never work out until we became "the three of us." That's the only way my world would get back to normal with a beach and friends of my own.

CHAPTER FOUR

✳

Contact

At the end of the eighth day, the lineup made contact. The two girls that did the first walk-by were different shades of blonde. They walked two feet in front of me, side-by-side, arm-in-arm, in the same rhythm. One of them wore a home-made Pier One Indian bikini and a straw hat. She had long wavy hair and cute cho cho Mick Jagger lips. She was eating a stalk of celery and holding a sparkling cold can of Tab. Her voice was so loud and raspy I could hear it over a siren ripping up PCH. She talked about going to see Led Zeppelin in Long Beach next week while the other one listened.

The girl listening was more of the Joni Mitchell type, wearing a Karenina bikini from Malibu. She had a slight overbite, a big smile, high lip line, and small white teeth that were perfectly aligned. An unlit cigarette dangled from her hand, and she had blonde highlights streaked evenly around her narrow face and halfway down her back. She had a high ribcage, tiny waist, and no hips and when she walked by, she gave me a slight nod. The other girl just stared at me and talked about Robert Plant originally wanting to name the band Mad Dogs.

After that walk-by, I knew they'd be doubling back soon. I had to get prepared. I reviewed in my mind the twenty-five most important rules:

1. **Always warn your friends when a surfer is close.**
2. **Girls don't fight with girls.**
3. **Do not wear a matching bikini unless you are a local and never wear the same color as someone already on the beach.**
4. **Never touch a surfer's board unless he hands it to you.**
5. **Be respectful of locals and high-ranking girls.**
6. **Everything you wear will be judged and inspected. Find your own style and stick to it.**
7. **Never cut your hair.**
8. **Never use nasty words in front of guys—they hate trash mouths.**
9. **Never go all the way with a surfer before you are officially his girlfriend or you will end up with a bad reputation.**
10. **It's better to die than to fart or barf.**
11. **Never talk in bathroom stalls.**
12. **Flush before you pee unless you're with the lineup. Then you must pee in front of them or they won't trust you.**
13. **Never look directly at a surfer when he's surfing. It could jinx him.**
14. **Always have a bathing suit with you.**

15. Don't ever talk about world events, politics, or money. Surfers hate brainy girls.
16. Keep your nails long for tickling. Surfers love to be tickled.
17. Bodysurfing is okay if the guys are out of the water.
18. Don't gulp or burp when you're drinking beer.
19. Always carry money. Most surfers don't pay for anything.
20. Never date a guy smaller than you.
21. Never flick sand on someone you want to be friends with.
22. Showing up on time is lame.
23. Never wear bright colors like pink, orange, or lime green.
24. Check your nose for snot drips before coming out of the water.
25. Be sincere.

On the way back from their walk, the girls came to the edge of my towel. I made a mental note that one wore a tiny checkered print bikini and the other wore a tapestry cloth. They were impressively skimpy bathing suits, but I'd seen smaller and hopefully someday they would, too. When I made local-girl status, I had to remember not to wear their colors or prints. That was forbidden. But I had a string bikini that I would wear someday and blow their minds.

"Hi. I'm Lisa H.," said the one with the overbite and checkered Karenina bikini.

Up close, she looked amazing. Her nose was a cute little button and her body was perfect. She had put on round, red-tinted sunglasses that edged down her face.

"I'm Lisa Y.," said the other one.

I tried not to make a face as Lisa Y.'s raspy voice pounded past me. What were the odds of both of them being named Lisa? I couldn't tell if they were putting me on.

"Do you have a match?" Lisa H. asked. I flicked open my lighter without a second thought, and she cupped her hands around mine to shield the flame. Her skin was soft and smelled like rose water.

After she took a deep inhale and blew the smoke directly in my face, she said, "So who are you?"

My dad named me after his favorite singer, Haunani Kahalewai, but there was no way these two *haole* beasts would ever be able to pronounce my full name, no matter how carefully I said it. So I told them, "Nani."

That meant "beautiful" in Hawaiian.

I took a deep breath and waited. There was a long silence. Then Lisa Y. asked, "Where you from?"

Kaimuki was too complicated so I simplified it and told them, "Honolulu."

"Cool," they said and walked away.

I waited until the Lisas were back at State before I dipped my hand under my towel and pulled out my M&Ms. My heart was still pounding.

I remembered Annie laughing as she gave me her jacket and told me about all the surfers she had kissed. She had sewn a puka shell on for each guy. But she warned me with a stern voice that, just the same, the most important rule was:

Never marry a surfer.

"They're no good for that," she said.

"Why?" I asked.

There were lots of reasons: surfers smoked too much pot and were oversexed. They were lazy and generally only worked when they needed plane fare to Bali or Australia or somewhere else in the world that had big waves.

Annie put a small plastic container in my hands. It was the diaphragm she'd used only once because she was on the pill. She said she thought it would probably fit me and suggested I keep it handy. It seemed that surfers like girls who looked sweet and young. I always hated my cute looks, but I guess they were finally going to work for me.

"Whatever you do," Annie warned, "don't let them know you're only fifteen. If you get asked your age, tell them you're a sophomore."

That suited me just fine. I didn't want them to know I skipped a grade anyway. My reputation for being smart shouldn't follow me to the mainland. Being smart was like the opposite of being popular. Besides, the only reason I skipped first grade was a scam anyway. After naptime one afternoon, I told my kindergarten teacher Miss Meli some stuff I memorized. I used to eavesdrop on the customers at my dad's bar. I just sort of blurted out: Earth Day was April 22; Spiro Agnew's middle name was Theodore and before he was vice president he was governor of Maryland; Thomas

Jefferson's face is on the nickel; Diamond Head in Hawaiian means "tuna forehead"; and Jupiter, Saturn, Uranus, and Neptune are the four planets in our solar system with gas in them. Poor Miss Meli had to sit down when I told her that napalm was made out of gasoline, soap, and aluminum and that it was (I spelled it for her) h-y-d-r-o-p-h-o-b-i-c, which meant it didn't stick to water. A short time after that I found myself in second grade.

Annie's image drifted away as I put my head down on my towel and sunk into the warm afternoon sand. The sound of small waves reminded me of the Kahala Gardens where I dreamt of getting married. The dream was perfect: I was becoming Mrs. Gerry Lopez at the wedding of the century. I wore a satin lace gown and the setting sun was making the sky an orange color. There was this big spread of sushi like the rich Japanese girls from Punahou had at their weddings and the entertainment came from *The Danny Kaleikini Show*. After the ceremony I would be known as Mrs. Pipeline, wife of the cutest surfer in the world. We would honeymoon at the Kahala Hilton, make out on the tiny couches in the elevators, drink champagne from etched crystal glasses, and sleep in crisp white sheets with double orchid vanda leis all around us. Gerry would buy me diamonds as big as gumballs and Annie Iopa would tell me, "That guy is okay."

CHAPTER FIVE

The DMZ

After ten days in LA, I could almost tolerate the murky cold ocean in Santa Monica. Thanks to The Turtles, I was learning how to navigate the rip tides and avoid the troublesome ditches. All I had to do was dodge the kids zipping across the wet sand on plywood skim boards and force myself to swim twice a day. The Turtles were very nice. They kept an eye on me and taught me everything I needed to know about their ocean.

The Jetty, I discovered, was just a boogie board beach with no real surfers and a lot less pressure. Even though the beaches were less than a mile apart, the waves broke smaller there than they did at State. It was easy to drop into the little curls, get some speed, and pull out. I bodysurfed, but once in a while I'd just crouch under the waves. It felt like ice cream pouring over my head. My breath got shallow and when I popped up, I'd gasp for air. I had to remember that making sounds in the water was against Annie's rules.

I wish I could have brought my records and turntable to the beach. The weekdays would've been a lot less lonely if I could have stuck my headphones on and disappeared into the music of Loggins & Messina, Procol Harem, Leon Russell, and The Moody Blues. I loved The Moody Blues. They played at The Shell once and hung out at my dad's bar. Dad's bar was famous in Honolulu. Everyone from Elvis, Elizabeth Taylor, Don Knotts, and Connie Stevens went there when they visited the island. They all loved the Java Jones 'cause it wasn't a tourist joint. It was the real deal. It had authentic tiki poles, a lava rock waterfall, fire dancers, and huge saltwater aquariums with hundreds of fish I personally named. But what it was most known for was its strong drinks and great music. Kui Lee and Tommy Sands got their starts there. So did the new singing duo Cecilio and Kapono. Dad said they were going to be big.

Every night, I sat at the end of the bar with my *Legends of Hawaii* coloring book listening for new facts to impress Miss Meli. Drunk people talk a lot. From the sailors and marines, I heard about the Viet Cong, air reconnaissance, draft resisters, Canada, Ho Chi Minh, the 17th parallel, and the demilitarized zones, also known as the DMZ.

State had a DMZ of its own. From a distance, I could see the boundary between the surfing side and the homosexual side of the beach. It was the first time the visible line of demarcation separating State Beach into two halves was clear to me. There was a zone about five feet wide that was clearly the DMZ because no one sat there. It looked like there were more than a hundred gay guys on the far side of it lying out on the beach. Surfers were notorious for hating gay men. It didn't matter what coast, continent, or island I was on, it was always the same. They called them *mahus* and thought they were the scum of the earth. I liked gay guys. Dad said gays and *Funny Kines* had a special magic. *Funny Kines* was the pidgin phrase for gay girls. Mom thought pidgin was for barbarians. Anyway, I think gays are a gift from Pele to balance the planet, but no way would I ever, ever actually say that out loud.

I was so busy looking at two muscle men rubbing oil on each other I didn't notice her shadow until it fell over me, blocking the sun. The Wild Card Girl was standing above me. She was twirling her long curly hair and her fingertips were pink from taking the shells off pistachio nuts. I only know that because she tossed one at me to get my attention. Her sunburned shoulders were even pinker than her fingertips. She sat on the end of my towel without asking. She was covered in freckles. I'd never seen so many before. She had them on her arms, her back, even on her pierced ears with giant hoops. But I liked her plum-colored bikini.

The Wild Card Girl wore too much jewelry for the beach. She had mood rings on every finger, bracelets crawling up her forearm, and at least four necklaces that were all twisted up from wearing them in the ocean.

"You're Nani, right?" she asked. I nodded.

"I'm Mary Jo Stevens. Leo," she said.

That explained why she was so bossy and territorial. It also meant she'd do anything to get her ego stroked.

"What sign are you?"

"Virgo."

"Can I have a sip?" she asked as she reached over and grabbed Dad's thermos. She twisted it open and chugged. Her face went bright red and she shook her head from side to side. Her brown gnome-like eyes got bigger and bigger. It was first time since my dad had his heart attack that I laughed.

"Vodka?" she asked.

I smiled and nodded again. She probably thought I was a party girl, which was fine with me. It would work in my favor. She didn't need to know I'd never had a drink in my life.

"Can I have more?" Mary Jo asked.

She took another chug. The more she drank, the happier she got. She leaned across my towel and offered me some pistachios. I don't like the pink kind, but refusing them, and a Leo, would have been a mistake for sure.

CHAPTER SIX

Baja Banquet

Mary Jo leaned in a little and adjusted her bikini so no tan lines showed. A beach conversation with a girl like this was a lot like surfing. You needed patience and had to get to the right spot at exactly the right moment before you took off.

"I like the puka shells in your hoops," she said.

"They're from Pipeline," I replied matter-of-factly.

"Bonsai?" she confirmed.

I got a twinge of satisfaction knowing Mary Jo was trying to impress me with her simple *haole* understanding of Pipeline, the greatest surfing spot on Earth. The way she said Bonsai was so touristy I almost started to laugh. Mary Jo leaned closer. I could smell Prell shampoo and Coppertone. I had her all lined up. Slowly, I pulled a Polaroid Annie gave me out of my suede tote bag and put it in Mary Jo's hands. It was of Gerry Lopez standing with Jeff Hakman, the *haole* local.

"This was when they were at Punahou, a fancy private school back home," I said.

Mary Jo stared at the two famous surfers.

"They don't get along anymore," I said.

Then I waited, watching Mary Jo. You see, I knew Gerry Lopez and Jeff were both Scorpios. They were way too intense to be friends. That sign is the most dangerous one in the zodiac. It always has its tail curved up, ready to strike.

I could tell Mary Jo was really impressed but trying to act cool. She handed the picture back to me and watched as I casually tossed it into my purse. I offered her one of my Lark 100s and lit it with Annie Iopa's Zippo lighter, the one made of abalone and silver. Mary Jo was blown away but continued to sit still and be quiet. She scanned down the beach for the lineup and stared at their hazy contours. She dabbed on a little lip gloss and then offered it to me. It was strawberry flavored and had melted from the heat—yuck. But like the pistachios, I had to accept it.

"Can you keep a secret?" Mary Jo whispered, looking around.

Secret was my middle name. Virgos love secrets. Secrets are doorways to power and keeping them is the best way to prove loyalty to a Leo. If I could get Mary Jo to trust me, anything was possible.

I raised my eyebrows, knowing this would encourage her to continue. Mary Jo looked like a lopsided rocket about to launch. She took my little finger into hers and made me swear I would never tell anyone what she was about to say. I swore. It was cute, making a pinkie oath with this chick. We sat face to face, cross-legged, like we were going to have a staring contest. I didn't question why she wanted to tell me a secret; I just listened to her talk.

"My brother Ray took me on a dawn patrol to Country Line the day before he shipped out to 'Nam," she said. "I had just gotten my braces off but had to wear a headgear. It was so disgusting. That's why I never left the back of the van and that's why I know what I know."

I waited with anticipation. Leos love to be center stage, and Mary Jo looked like she was enjoying every moment. Like a lioness that had been starved for years and was finally getting a piece of meat. She gave me a wicked glance and continued, "Not long ago, Roxanne West, a.k.a. Rox or Rocks, the one with the gigantic jugs, get it, Rocks? Anyway, her and Claire Carlson, her copilot, you know, the one with the straight, long, blonde hair, the one who wears turquoise all the time? Anyway, they had so-so status at State until The Baja Banquet."

So, Miss Macadamia was Rox and Lemon Verbena was Claire. The fact that they were once "wannabes" was important insider information. Mary Jo stared harder into my eyes, blinking maybe once or twice. I had to look respectful as she went on. I, too, tried not to blink, knowing that was a sign of weakness.

"It all began when a Category 5 hurricane hit Cabo San Lucas. There were these really high surf warnings and every guy with a board waited for Baja to get totaled. The next morning, County Line was a full-on zoo before the sun even came up. Rox and Claire had a primo parking spot so every hottie in the water could see them."

I knew the funny thing about being a surf groupie was no one could know you were one. So, I had to ask Mary Jo, "How did they just hang out?"

Mary Jo purposefully rolled her eyes and started shoot-
ing off information like her mouth was a machine gun and
every word was a bullet.

"Rox and Claire turned themselves into these, like,
weather forecasters. They could tell you anything about tide
changes, barometer readings, and all kinds of weather stuff.
That's how they got on all the beaches."

Very clever, I thought as Mary Jo took a breath and
rattled on.

"The only other girls on the beach were from Topanga.
They stink of patchouli and dress like gypsies. They've got
hippie parents who let them grow and sell pot. And peyote
buttons by the milk bottle. Surfers love them."

That's one hell of a way to earn an allowance, I thought.
My dad grew pot, but it was off-limits to me. I only started
smoking cigarettes the day after he died. Screw it, I had
thought. Mary Jo continued on with the story. "Ray wedged
his van into the spot next to Rox and Claire by taking the
front fender off the car behind him. To this day, Rox and
Claire still don't know I was in the back of his van. Claire
was, ya know, going for one of the foxy born-again twins,
Shawn McBride."

Mary Jo took another long gulp of the Daddy-tini and
paused. "*McBride*," she said emphatically, "you know, Nixon's number one backer? You know what I'm talking about?"

Mary Jo must have thought we didn't get the news in
Hawaii. She looked at me like maybe I didn't know who the
president was. Duh. The first thing my mom did when we
got to our new house was register her Republican ass at the

post office so she could vote for Dick in November. Mary Jo lifted her arms and stretched up to the sky and yawned. It was as though she was remembering for the first time exactly what happened.

"It was 6:39 a.m. and just a regular two- to three-foot morning. Nothing special about the surf until these lines started swelling on the horizon. You know, big waves don't ever appear on cue, but these babies were sneaking in just below the skyline. Surfers in the take-off zone couldn't see them coming. I could hardly believe it. These waves were going to be, like, triple over-headers with a thirteen foot drop."

I knew calling in a motherload at a hot surf spot was like becoming Miss America. For a girl, it meant instant fame.

I had to ask, "How did they get everyone's attention?"

Mary Jo made a sweeping gesture with her arm, waving and shaking her head. She was truly the most dramatic Leo I had ever met.

"They couldn't at first," she said. "The guys in the takeoff zone were too far out. The lines were coming in so fast Rox and Claire had to do something radical. And what they did turned them into legends. It was Rox who came up with the plan: to do a full-on, doubleheader flash. She was already kind of historical for her boobs, but because she had a good girl reputation, like, none of the guys had actually seen them. That meant a quick flash was their duty. But Claire was chicken. You know, she went to Corpus Christi, that Catholic school in Pacific Palisades? And she was so scared that her mom would find out. Rox finally asked her, 'What's the worst thing that could happen? You never play paddle tennis at the Bel-Air Bay Club again?'"

Mary Jo stopped and ate a couple pistachios, carefully removing each from its shell. I mean, untangling a ball of yarn would have been easier than figuring out how long it was gonna take for her to spill exactly what happened. Mary Jo was like an old Hawaiian storyteller. She took her time to re-create each moment with specific details that only she knew about. Stuff like the fact that Claire was drinking a strawberry Slimfast and that they always liked to perch under the sign on Tongo Street, in the same spot so the guys would recognize them. And that they blasted Humble Pie like it was their theme band so everyone on PCH could hear it.

"Rox was, like, going crazy trying to convince Claire to flash. She jumped up and down, clenched her fists, bit her lip she was so angry. Finally, out of nowhere, she farted."

Mary Jo started laughing and slapped her thigh. She pushed her elbow into my side, and I knew that was my cue to start laughing, too. As I did, I thought about that rule: *it's better to die than to fart.* Mary Jo was still laughing as she said, "Rox gave Claire that look. You know that 'it wasn't me' look? And the next thing she says, Rox that is, 'On the count of three . . . ready . . . one, two, two and a half . . .' Somehow Rox farting gave Claire the edge she needed. Claire couldn't wait another second and blurted out, 'Three!'"

"What happened next?" I asked.

Mary Jo was laughing so hard she could barely talk.

"So they stood there topless. It was silent, like they were standing over an open grave. All I heard was whitewash below and a dog barking down the beach. They were point-ing toward the oncoming line of waves, waiting for someone to notice them. They started to panic, and that's when I covered my eyes."

It sounded awful. The sun was baking into my back, but I knew better than to move.

"How could they flash a packed Sunday crowd and live?" I asked Mary Jo.

"That's a good question," she said patting my shoulder. "After a few seconds, I heard a hoot coming from the water. I flipped back the curtains of the van to see Jerry Richmond waving both his arms over his head. I mean, that guy is so mellow he barely talks so to see him all excited was, like, a really big deal. The roar that followed sounded like a Who concert when the lights go out.

"Surfers piled up and paddled out so fast, making so much noise, the bikers at Neptune's Net, who were still drinking from the night before, came charging across PCH, probably thinking they'd get to see something cool like a dead surfer or beached whale. So, you know what happened next?"

I shook my head no, keeping my posture tall and straight.

Mary Jo continued, "Every surfer from San Diego to Swami's and all the way past Rincon heard about the call Rox and Claire made, and from that day on, they became the gnarliest girls to ever walk the beach."

With that, Mary Jo took a slight bow. Of course, I applauded as she finished the story.

"Rox and Claire never bragged about what locals called The Baja Banquet. Surfers just decided they were lucky charms and that changed their status forever."

Mary Jo told me about girls foolish enough to try and talk to Rox or Claire. Seemed they would freeze the girls out. They'd stand there, not talking, with their arms crossed and little smiles on their faces. If the girls tried to break the ice, they'd just stare at them harder, happy to know they could freak chicks out and get a tan at the same time.

"You know, I really hate them," Mary Jo said. She stood up, staring at the ocean, swaying with the tide. I settled back down on my towel, trying to look normal and relaxed; I rolled over onto one side and rested my head in the palm of my hand, waiting.

"Do you want to meet them?" she asked.

I wanted to say "Hell no" and start swimming home to Oahu, but instead I said, "For sure."

Mary Jo's arms loosened and her shoulders rolled in. I could tell she was relieved.

"Great. Stop by tomorrow," she said as she started jogging in place.

I could see the muscles in her calves flex. She must have been really good at volleyball because even drunk she could sail on top of the sand. I wanted to ask her what time, but I knew it was a lame question so I just smiled. She started jogging backwards. "Make sure you have something for Lord Ricky," she said, pointing her finger at me. Before I could ask, she turned and yelled back over her shoulder, "He guards State's entrance. And watch out for the gargoyles that work for him."

She waved. "Don't worry. I'll tell them you're coming," she said and started to jog away. Then she came back once more to tell me, "Oh yeah, Suzie and Jenni are best friends, Aries and Libra. And KC sits on the last towel, Aquarius."

And with that she plowed down the beach once and for all.

Leos always had an agenda but it didn't matter. I really liked Mary Jo. I waited until the lineup had packed up and left before I headed home. I had to shave my legs, arms, and my underarms. Most importantly, I had to write Annie and tell her what had just happened. She was going to be stoked.

CHAPTER SEVEN

※

Bad Cow

I could tell Mom was home from work. I heard that obnoxious song, "American Pie," blasting out the kitchen window.
I hated it when my mom used my record player. She already
ruined the needle, picking it up and slamming it down, listening to Don McLean's song over and over. What kind of
an idiot writes a song about a bunch of people dying? The
lyrics always got stuck in my head. This is the day that I
die—you die, we die, my dad dies. "This'll be the day that
I die," was the exact quote. It was all the same to me but
not for my mom. She believed the song had a secret message about Jesus's resurrection, and she was determined to
decode it.

I could also tell, from the smell of grated orange peels,
chopped nuts, and butter, that she was baking the cookies
she always made. I didn't have to see my mother to know
she'd be wearing a floral muumuu patio dress with the deep
side pockets filled with used tissues and a pack of Benson &
Hedges. Underneath, she'd have on Lollipop white panties
with a control top waist and crossover bra with a double

back hook. She'd be barefoot or wearing ballet slippers, and if she had already showered, she would have an ugly orange scarf covering up the curlers in her hair. I walked through the door ready for the stink of Aqua Net and cheap white wine. I slowed down to enjoy my last minutes of freedom and took a few deep breaths of fresh air. Mom didn't believe in astrology. She thought it was stupid and superstitious. I had to rely on moment-to-moment observations to make sense of her, even though she was a Virgo like me.

My mom used to look like the photo of Yvette Mimieux on the cover of *LIFE* magazine. I saved that October 1963 issue because inside it showed pictures of her—Yvette, not my mother, learning how to surf. My mom looked so much like her that people used to stop and ask her for an autograph. Dad thought that was hot. He loved blondes and said he and my mom were like sweet and sour, yin and yang. He always said opposites attract. Those were in the good old days when she went tide pooling and rafting with me. When she used to sit on a little chair next to my bed if I was sick, comb my hair a hundred times at night, and sing along with The Mamas & The Papas. But now that she was a widow, everything had changed.

In Hawaii, she and Dad did their own thing, but they'd always come together at the bar. She would supervise the hostesses and name all the drinks. Dad would do the hiring and firing, and I would be responsible for picking out the fish and naming them all. Everybody got along back then. When Mom got too serious, Dad would always find a way to make her laugh.

As I walked up to our new house, I remembered where I was; my stomach turned. Mom peered at me like I was a science project that had just grown mold. She signaled for me to use the garden path, which wasn't really a path—just a bunch of uneven cement slabs on a hillside of overgrown vines, succulent plants, donkey tails, ferns, and gnarled bougainvillea. Mom's garden was one of the highlights of our new home at 33 Sage Street, which was more an alley than a street and was buried deep in the Santa Monica Canyon below white adobe homes on a winding road called Amalfi Drive.

My mom chose 33 Sage for us to start a new life because she thought it was the greatest house in the world and just the place where Dad would want us to be. I think she wanted off the rock, a.k.a. Hawaii, and back on the clock. Mom was excited to be living on the mainland again.

There was hamburger meat on the counter next to an open box of Rice-A-Roni, an MJB coffee can with some bacon grease, Tabasco sauce, and a bunch of stained recipes. Mom walked toward me with a tray of freshly baked nut cookies. Her upper lip curled as she said, "Your favorite," shoving the biggest one in my mouth.

That was her way of trying to shut me up and stop a fight before it started. But I wasn't interested in a fight right then. The only thing that interested me was meeting Rox and Claire and there was no way I was going to tell my mother that.

Two new fake mahogany plastic TV trays were set up in front of the old Zenith.

"Those are cool," I said.

"Dinner will be at six." The way Mom said it was as if she was saying, "See, everything is just as it was before Dad's heart attack." But it wasn't.

I closed the bathroom door, stuck a towel in my mouth, and screamed. *If only I had a brother or sister,* I thought, *it wouldn't be so terrible. At least I'd have somebody to talk to about what was going on.* But I only had a "bad cow" to lean on. That's what my mom called herself when she couldn't make breast milk or have another child. I swear to God she told anyone who would listen that she was a "bad cow." What a freak.

Seeing those TV trays, I finally got the picture. I was living with an android: a nonhuman Stepford Mom who floated through life as if my dead father was on a fishing trip or something. From the top of her blonde hair to her manicured toenails, my mother had been transformed by Miltown prescriptions and white wine into a person I didn't recognize, didn't like, and who I will refer to as Jean from now on.

CHAPTER EIGHT

✳

33 Sage

The bathroom at 33 Sage Street has a nauseating smell left by the old lady who used to live here. She kept all kinds of stuff under the sink like her cat's litter box, talcum powder, and Vicks VapoRub. Combined with the toxic fumes from three layers of paint applied by Jean, the smell was enough to make me want to use the hose to shower outside.

The paint was a creamy color that Jean thought was a great accent for the black and pink tiles. She had taken down the blinds and put up lacy curtains to make the bathroom more feminine. She also put in a no-slip white vinyl floor to make the tiny room look bigger and a heater to make it warmer.

Dad hated pink. I missed him so much and wished I could hear his voice or see him one more time. I dreamed of when we hiked the far side of Diamond Head. I liked to think he was still there with his biceps as round as coconuts, his deep voice, and his face reeking of Alpine aftershave. He'd be wearing his favorite Sandy Beach tank top and "sleepahs." The gap between his front teeth was just like mine, and his long salt-and-pepper hair made him look like his hero, Duke Kahanamoku, who was such a great surfer and Olympic swimmer he was known as The Human Fish. Duke Kahanamoku was super good-looking and so was my dad with his wide, flat nose and cool sideburns.

Our hiking time was special. When we were on the trail, he opened up and told me all about spirituality. His thick eyebrows arched up when he talked about *Kumulipo*, the creation chant.

"Everything happened after darkness," he said. "And a bunch of gods came to earth with light."

Stuff like that. It was so boss. He was so proud of our heritage.

Dad also showed me how to barbeque Spam, shop at the swap meet in Pearl City, roll super-tight joints for his morning toke, and most importantly, how to be silent so I could hear the wind and listen to what the ancestors said. I never actually heard them talk but my dad said they were there and that was good enough for me.

It was obvious that Dad was a Taurus by the sound of his voice. It was like sweet music. He was the kind of guy that stuck to his routine. Every day he got up at 10:00 a.m., had his protein drink and a joint, went for a swim, got a *poi* or a fish taco, and then went to the Java Jones. Tauruses are earth signs; they have deep roots connected to the places they live and the family they love. My dad also cared about the people he worked with. But mostly he was a really easygoing guy who just liked to sit in the sun at the beach for hours.

Dad loved *pakalolo,* and since we had a little house on lots of land in Kaimuki, he grew the pot in our backyard. There was so much of it he could pick it from the kitchen window. We had no screens so geckos came inside. I wanted them as pets but that made Jean crazy. Dad actually had to put up an electric "lizard zapper" to calm her down. She'd rather hear them sizzle than see them leisurely cruise around the house. That's the kind of person I live with.

I didn't want to think about Jean. I needed to get ready for my big day tomorrow. I covered my face with Noxzema and, just to be safe, covered it with Clearasil right afterward. My hair had to be perfectly straight and my skin had to be pimple free. For good luck, I rubbed my rabbit foot and dabbed the gardenia oil Annie gave me under my feet, around each toenail, and behind my ears. I wasn't about to leave a single beauty tip unturned.

Jean's loud knock startled me.

"Do you want cheese on your burger?" she shouted.

"No thanks," I said.

"Well, hurry up in there. It's almost six."

Jean was worried I'd miss the news about Nixon and the Watergate break-in. I swear she cared more about Nixon than me and really only wanted me there so she had someone to talk to. Jean loved to talk, especially about my going to Smith someday just like Julie Nixon. God forbid I ended up selling hot dogs at the North Shore like some crazed island girl or worse, getting married to a *Moke* who lived in the back woods. In the old days, whalers called big Hawaiian men who couldn't speak English *Moke*. It's not a nice word, and I hated it when Jean used it to try and act cool. That just made me spit.

My room was the worst part of 33 Sage. It had floral wall-paper, a pegboard, and a built-in plastic desktop that Jean called, "the hobby area." Like I had a friggin' hobby. There were two small windows with lacy curtains that Jean bought at Henshey's Department Store, a door to the bathroom, and a mattress directly in the middle of the room. Jean had unpacked and placed everything just where she thought it should be, including a wooden cross, a picture of Jesus with bloody palms opened to the sky, and a rosary right in the middle of my wall. I hated the place from top to bottom. The only good thing was that I could hear the ocean at night, and that made it easy for me to drift off to sleep.

Jean's dream was to live in a house with wall-to-wall shag carpeting. She had the floors at 33 Sage covered in mallard green shag. She chose that color because she saw in a celebrity magazine that Jack Lord had it in his Kahala condominium and she wanted just what that *haole* geek with the bad toupee had. How lame was that? It was just one more thing that made the entire house look awful and like we had lived in it for years.

Jean's room was once the den. She painted it god-awful mauve. She was crazy for these bifolding shutter closet doors. She had two panel mirrors installed so she could make sure her nursing uniform didn't show a panty line. The sliding glass doors led to the overgrown ravine, which she referred to as "her garden." Outside, there was a clothesline and white wicker chairs with paint chipping off and a hibachi. Although she had big plans for the place, it was a mess.

In the living room, there were a couple of bookshelves filled with Jean's paperbacks. *Jonathan Livingston Seagull* and

Valley of the Dolls were jammed between seashells she picked up over the years. When I was younger, instead of sucking my thumb, I used to stick my tongue in her cowry shells and lick the pink tinges with deep folds. The thick, solid shells had wavy notches that opened into rippled panels. Sometimes I would lick them until my mouth went raw. Weird as it was, those shells were my thing.

Jean loved the living room's fireplace. It was warm, but I didn't think it was a good idea for her to be starting fires after downing four or five tumblers of wine. On the mantel there was a framed picture of me on Dad's shoulders on Easter Sunday when I was four. I was wearing a cardigan over a polka-dot skirt with a silk bow on the side. He was wearing red and white floral trunks. Next to it was the wedding picture of Jean and my dad barefoot in a tuxedo when they were madly in love. Dad's ultimate favorite photo was of me getting hugged by Duke Kahanamoku, grinning ear to ear in front of his surfboards on the beach at Waikiki.

By the time I walked into the kitchen, Jean was taking our plates to the new TV trays. She had painted the whole kitchen blue and white to match her treasured Poppytrail dishes. Everything in that kitchen for serving food—from the salt and pepper shakers and the creamer to the sugar bowl and the gravy boat—was Poppytrail. The design was of little blue Dutch girls and boys under windmills. The place felt like a Poppytrail gift store. But oddly enough those dishes were the only things that made 33 Sage feel like home.

I ate dinner wearing my flannel nightgown, Hawaii State sweatshirt with the hood over my head, and thermal socks.

"You look like you're ready for snow," Jean laughed.

"It's freezing," I said.

From the Zenith, Walter Cronkite's familiar voice belted out, "Good Evening."

I couldn't have cared less what he said, and I wasn't about to have a pointless conversation with Jean about the climate in Santa Monica. I stuffed a spoonful of Green Giant corn into my mouth and wondered if Dad ever ate off of this plate.

CHAPTER NINE

Uncle Mike

I had to focus and get a good night's sleep. If I screwed up my first meeting with the lineup, I'd live alone in surf purgatory for the rest of my life.

One big problem was that Mary Jo never said what time I should stop by. If I showed up too early, they'd definitely think I was uncool. And for sure I'd blow it if I showed up too late. That would look like I didn't care.

I had to be prepared with answers to every question they could throw my way. If they asked who my favorite movie stars were I'd tell them Ali MacGraw, Robert Redford, and Paul Newman. If they asked, *Butch Cassidy and the Sundance Kid* was my favorite movie. Those were perfect answers because they were safe.

Actually, my favorite movie was *Barbarella* with Jane Fonda. When I was eleven, Uncle Mike had a private screening of it at his house. My folks thought I was asleep on the *lanai* but I saw the whole movie. Barbarella screwed an angel, played in sexy machines, and went to a dream chamber. That's where the Great Tyrant, Anita Pallenberg, sort of "did it" with Jane Fonda. That was my favorite part. The Tyrant was so hot. I wanted an eye patch like her to act all "pretty pretty" someday.

I could watch *Barbarella* every night, but telling that to the lineup was way too risky. Especially since Anita P. was my role model. That chick was slick, totally tough and ready to whip her way to the top, like me. Like I said, back home, girls who "did it" with girls were called *Funny Kines.* I don't think *Funny Kines* are creepy like gym teachers, nuns, or Joan Baez. To me, *Funny Kines* are beautiful like Barbarella.

The phone rang. Jean shot me a look like I knew who was calling so late. *Be serious*, I thought. *I don't have any friends in California.*

"Well, it's not for me," I said. Jean picked up the receiver.

"Hello. Oh Mike, is that you?"

She put her hand over her chest and fell back on the couch as if she had never gotten a long distance phone call before.

"It's Uncle Mike," Jean whispered, covering the receiver with her palm.

I liked Uncle Mike, but he had gotten way too chummy with Jean since Dad died. Not like they were together or anything, but something about their new friendship bugged me. They talked day and night.

Uncle Mike was Dad's business partner. His full name was Michael Kei. Dad always said Mike's only vices were tailored silk shirts from Singapore, tall blondes who liked to party, and four packs of Lucky Strikes a day. Uncle Mike was only five-foot-four in his slip-on loafers, but his ego was huge, and his house was even bigger. On his mailbox in front of the long drive leading down to his private beach was the Hawaiian word *kahuna,* which means "king."

Uncle Mike bought up land in Kahala when it was nothing but pig farms. He turned it into multimillion-dollar estates and made so much dough Dad used to say that the title *Kahuna* actually fit him. You see, Uncle Mike's a bubbly Aries. "Generous to a fault," he'd tell you.

I loved Uncle Mike's house with its tennis court, pool, sleek marble floors, weird Eames furniture, and black lacquered counters. Best of all were his two Hyacinth macaws from Bolivia, Sonny and Cher. When anyone tried to figure out how he got those birds into the country, Dad would grin.

"Uncle Mike is resourceful," he'd say.

Jean hated "the birds," which is probably why I loved them so much. The night Sonny bit the nose of an overly friendly guest, she said they were "hideous creatures" and "filthy beasts." Jean threw up when Sonny flipped the fleshy chunk of skin in the air and swallowed it whole. All I could do was laugh and think about what a badass that bird was. Dad thought it was funny, too. "Ain't no big thang," he told Jean.

Dad always thought the things Mom got upset about were funny. "Opposites attract, and then one of them gets pregnant," Dad told me. Jean didn't think that was funny either.

She pushed away the TV tray, listening to Uncle Mike, slowly drawing each word out into a question. She said, "Really? Really? Really?"

"What?" I mouthed.

Like I was the little maid, Jean handed me her plate to clear. I rolled my eyes and wondered if she had completely lost it. Jean made me super stressed, but stress causes zits so I sucked it up. *Think smart and just play along with her*, I told myself. The lineup was the only thing that mattered.

I set the plates down in the kitchen. Jean kept a lot of liquor in there: vodka, rum, brandy, tequila, scotch, dry gin. The brandy was for making Fog Cutters, and the dry gin was for Singapore Slings. The bottles reminded me of Dad. I took a deep breath of vodka, clanged the bottles together, and started to clean up.

I could hear Jean babbling to Uncle Mike. She would talk to him for hours because it was on his dime.

She told him, "I want to know everything."

She sounded excited. I didn't really care.

Jean hated Uncle Mike's new girlfriend, Bibi Caprice. She was from Scandinavia by way of Las Vegas. I'll never forget the way Jean groaned when she saw her at our going-away party. The chick towered over Uncle Mike by at least a foot. It was really twisted. Bibi had on black stiletto heels and a one-piece fishnet bathing suit cut so low her giant tits almost fell out.

"Thank God your father doesn't have to meet this one," Jean whispered. But I knew Daddy always got a kick out of Uncle Mike's dames. Trust me, he would have split his sides laughing at Bibi's boobs jiggling up next to Uncle Mike's ears.

Everybody on Oahu knew Uncle Mike. People loved to talk about him. The talk wasn't always good. They said he was in the back pocket of The Big Five. They were a bunch of rich *haole* families who owned more of Hawaii than the military ever would.

Even so, Daddy loved Uncle Mike. They grew up together and were best friends since the days they worked side by side as beach boys for the Royal Hawaiian. Daddy said Mike was a "good guy, a real *Kanaka*," even though he didn't approve of his friends or his plans to build up and down the coast. Uncle Mike was getting rich by developing thousands of acres of beachfront property into condominium complexes and hotels. "The unavoidable future of Oahu," Uncle Mike would say, and then he'd laugh about how every inch of the island would soon be covered with cement. Nobody else thought it was funny.

For some reason, talking to Uncle Mike was getting Jean all revved up. She sounded hysterical. When I went back into the living room, she was stomping her feet and squealing like she had swallowed air from a helium balloon. Then it got even weirder because she started chanting, "We're rich, we're rich," and couldn't stop. She had finally lost her mind.

Jean was laughing like I'd never heard her laugh before. She floated around the room holding onto the long phone cord.

"Mike, call me tomorrow," she said.

She was acting totally mondo bizarro, jumping up and down like a cheerleader, clapping her hands when she said, "Uncle Mike sold the bar."

She chirped in my face, smiling and shaking me as her hands clawed into my shoulders.

"What?" I asked, even though I knew exactly what she had said.

There was no way it could be true. Uncle Mike wouldn't sell the place and Jean couldn't do it without him. Everyone knew that Annie Iopa was running the Java Jones until I turned twenty-one, when I would legally take over. So it couldn't be sold. There was no way.

"We're rich, honey," Jean said. "Uncle Mike is cutting us a check tonight for one hundred thousand dollars."

Jean took my face in her hands and kissed my cheek. When I didn't respond, she snapped her fingers a few times around my head.

"Wake up!" she shouted. "Don't you get it? You can get braces now. You can go shopping and have a birthday bash at Trader Vics. We can even go to the Kahala Hilton someday and sit front row at the *Danny Kaleikini Show*."

I didn't say anything. "Why the stink face?" Jean asked. She sounded all surprised.

The inside of my throat closed, and my tongue felt too big for my mouth. I heard my heart pounding beneath my ears and a burst of heat rushed through me. There was no time to think. It had to be said, right then and there. The room was spinning. I could barely get enough air. But I had to say it and say it strong.

"The Jones is mine."

Jean laughed. She tried to make me laugh, too, twirling my hair and using it to make a pretend moustache across my face.

She said, "Honey, we'll be ladies of leisure."

She had no idea that I was boiling inside and that every move she made or word she uttered made me feel like my bones were being blown apart. The scent of her lipstick and ketchup on her breath were making me sick. She was still laughing but then, finally, she realized that I was for real.

"You're not even sixteen yet," she said. "We couldn't keep the bar, honey." She patted my arm and turned away.

It was the way Jean said "honey" that pushed me overboard. I liked it when my dad called me "honey," but Jean's tone made the word fester and stick like tar.

"We? Who said anything about you owning the bar? Daddy left me the Java Jones."

"Kids don't own bars," Jean laughed.

That bar was my ticket home. I wasn't about to lose it. I couldn't. It was my main tie to Dad, the only one I had except for his ashes. Annie was counting on me and, besides, all my tropical fish were still in the tanks.

Jean stepped away. There was no hint of a smile on her face anymore.

"How do you think we got this great house, huh?" She waited for me to answer but I had nothing to say. "Uncle Mike fronted us the money so we could have a place to live."

Again, she waited for me to say something. There was silence in the room, but the screaming in my head was epic until I finally said, "Get it back."

"No," she said.

"Get it back!" I yelled.

"No," she said.

"Daddy said it was going to be mine," I screamed.

I felt like I had stepped on a bomb and fell to the ground. I imagined my guts, fingers, and blood spewing into the air like fireworks on the Fourth of July. The last thing I wanted to do was cry, but I couldn't control myself. Tears streamed out of me and felt unstoppable. I shook, kicked, and scratched at the air, but Jean didn't seem to care.

"Here's the deal," she said calmly. "The bar is gone. Mike and I decided."

She stood there staring at me. I cried like I have never cried before. I wanted to yank her hair out, stomp on her head, crushing her brains with my bare feet.

"Honey, please. . ." Jean tried to touch me, but I slapped her hand away and crawled into a corner.

"I hate you, bitch," I said.

I had never sworn in front of my mother, let alone cursed at her.

She walked away. I stayed there, in the corner plotting my next move. This was not going to blow over, and I would never forgive her. It was not a little family feud, but a full-blown vendetta. I swore to myself, someday I'd get the bar back—somehow, someway.

In the meantime, I would make the rest of my mother's life a living hell. And I would follow every rule and regulation laid out by Annie Iopa to get in with the lineup. I was going to become the gnarliest girl on State Beach. That was my destiny. From now on, I would take no prisoners, show no mercy, and become a new legend in the world of surf. That way nobody would ever jerk me around again.

II

Iulai

July 1972

Leo

♌

CHAPTER TEN

Crossing Over

There was no trace of Jean when I woke up, but she had tacked another small picture of Jesus, this one with lambs, next to the cross on my wall. *A sign*, I thought. Today I needed all the help I could get. I didn't give a flying fig where it came from.

I reviewed my mission and pulled the covers over my head, closing my eyes tight. I wanted to make it dark and calm in my head. There was no turning back. I was marooned on the mainland permanently. The only thing left to do was erase that round little *Haunani* with too much "milk" in her dark *Kona* skin. The girl that played with Little Kiddles and dressed in muumuus that matched her mother's had to be banished forever.

I got out of bed, hugged Mrs. Beasley, and brushed my hair so it hung straight. Then I begged the great mother Pele on my knees, "Please make me cute, make me strong, and most of all make me cool."

Somehow the local girls were going to test me. I knew that because Annie Iopa told me what to expect. She also told me exactly how to respond.

"No matter what the challenge is," she said, "let the home girl win."

She looked directly into my eyes and said all seriously, "Just barely, but let her win. Understand?"

I nodded but didn't have any idea what she meant. Today I was going to find out.

To get onto State Beach, I had to get past Lord Ricky and his gargoyles. That's what Mary Jo called his sidekicks, the two guys that guarded the tunnel entrance. I had seen them and knew they'd be on watch with him. They'd all require payment of some kind. I had the perfect bribe: five excellent joints with no seeds.

I decided to keep wearing Annie's mismatched North Shore bikini. The one with the crocheted top that looked like a spider web and the black and white bikini bottoms. I looped my lucky rabbit foot around the side and tied my halter top good and tight. For extra mojo, I wrapped an oversized black and khaki bandana around my neck. A soldier at the bar had given it to me for good luck.

I wore drawstring shorts over my bikini bottoms and filled my suede tote with the necessities: a key to the house, a fold-up brush, a five-dollar bill, a butter and sugar sandwich on Wonder Bread, a thermos filled with vodka for good luck, cinnamon Fireballs, and the Band-Aid box filled with Dad, just in case they gave me permission to swim.

Finally, I put on the black wrap-around shades Mr. Ho gave me after Dad died. He told me I was beautiful and I could call if I ever needed anything. Don Ho liked *haole* women like my dad did so he thought I was the coolest. Jean called Don Ho tropical tacky and said he was Mister Kisser because he loved sucking face with old tourist women who stunk of gardenia perfume and Dole pineapple. They had one too many slushy bourbon drinks with double umbrellas in coconut shells. "Good for tips," Dad would say.

I popped one of Jean's Valiums and headed for the beach. She had offered them to me before, medicine to calm down. She had been trying to get me to calm down for a long time. Today I finally took her advice.

I estimated it took ten minutes to get from my house to the tunnels. I walked on West Channel Road past the famous Natural Progression, the number one surf shop, and got a couple hoots from the guys inside. That was a good sign. NP was the board mecca for locals. The further I got from 33 Sage, the deeper I was able to breathe, the clearer I was able to think, and the more confident I felt.

After crossing the street, just before the stairs down into the tunnel, I joined a pack of moms and little kids heading to State. I held hands with one of the little buckaroos while chatting with his mom about the possibility of a babysitting job I knew I'd never do.

At State's entrance, Lord Ricky was sitting on an upside-down garbage can. Before my feet touched the sand, he held up a golf club and stopped me. He let the moms and little kids pass but made me wait. He looked about twenty-five or so and wore plastic Mickey Mouse sunglasses, a yellow bathrobe that was too small, and white tennis shorts. Typical of surfers like him, a dark shadow was looming under the fabric, which meant no underwear. He had a giant hickey on his neck. He sat there, dripping wet and fastening a pith helmet under his scraggly beard. The guy was hard-core and most likely a Gemini.

"Young Lady," Lord Ricky sang, dragging out the "a" to make it sound like he had an English accent.

Guys don't like grumpy girls so I smiled. Lord Ricky dropped the golf club and let me step onto the beach. But I knew not to go farther.

My eyes drifted over to Lord Ricky's sidekicks. They were real *Blala,* lowlifes. Lord Ricky introduced me to them even though he didn't know my name. He put his arm over my shoulder and pulled me tight to his side. Pointing to one of the guys, he said, "This is Stu."

Stu was at least six feet tall and waddled like a big goose. He had a baby face, giant blue eyes, a booming deep voice, and was wearing Hang Ten trunks.

"How do you do?" he said and curtsied formally. It was the kind of thing an Aquarius might do, but I wasn't positive about him. I wasn't sure if I should curtsy back. So instead I just smiled bigger.

"And this . . . this is Mr. Brad Jackson," he offered up as though he were introducing someone famous.

Jean would have said Brad had a "misaligned eye." While his right eye looked straight ahead and focused, his left one wandered outward. This was my first real challenge of the day. I knew that eye contact was very important to surfers when it was allowed, but I didn't know which of his eyeballs to look at. I silently went through a round of eeny, meeny, miny, moes then picked the non-wandering eye and said, "Hi."

"These are my *brahs*," Lord Ricky told me.

It is so totally lame when *haoles* try to use pidgin or any kind of Hawaiian words.

Lord Ricky told me his *brahs* designed boards at Natural Progression and were part-time pool men for movie stars. Both guys stunk of chlorine, rubber, and disinfectant. They weren't the least bit wet, but the chemical combination made them shimmer in the late morning sun.

With his arm still around me, Lord Ricky blew a saliva bubble off the tip of his tongue. I stood perfectly still, trying to look unbreakable, as the little spit bubble floated by me. I wanted to rub my rabbit foot to get Annie praying for me, but I knew that any sudden movement could set them off. So I didn't try to make casual conversation. I just stood there and waited.

"Do you have an invitation?" Lord Ricky asked.

"Mary Jo," was all I said.

Lord Ricky dropped his arm around my waist and shook his head side to side.

"No," he said. "I need to *see* the invitation."

It sounded like he had marbles in his mouth when he talked. I dropped my eyes past his pigeon chest and stared at his knobby knees. Lord Ricky didn't say anything. I waited. If my dad was here, this wouldn't be happening. Lord Ricky would be chewing sand before he got a paw on me. I didn't move.

CHAPTER ELEVEN

※

Initiation I: Gargoyles

"Who are you?" Lord Ricky asked.

"Nani," I said calmly.

"Got a joint for me, chick-wa?" he said.

It wasn't really a question. The way he narrowed his eyes, rolled his tongue, and accented the "wa" transformed his speech into a warning. Lord Ricky coiled himself around me. Before I could give him a joint, he turned my bag upside down.

I knew better than to bend over around these guys but kneeling wasn't an option either. I didn't want to be face to face with their crotches. Squatting would make me look like I was peeing so I decided to perch myself like a tiny bird on the sand. I quickly scooped up the Band-Aid box, but before I could get up, Stu and Brad squeezed in next to me, sealing us all together.

"We wanna joint, too, chickie-poo," Brad said.

He had traces of zinc oxide around his nostrils and up close, I could smell his dog-mouth morning breath. Stu had a nicer edge to him. He just gave me a wink as I handed him a joint and put his arm around me, clicking his tongue in my ear.

"We wanna know your whole name," he said looking down at my boobs.

"*Haunani Nuuhiwa*, but call me Nani," I said just barely squeaking it out.

"How, Nani." Lord Ricky said like an Indian on *Gunsmoke.* He dropped his voice deeper and raised his arm with the palm of his hand open.

He made me the morning's "itty-bitty," the girl who either got her butt kicked or stayed and played. There was no in-between. Lord Ricky kneeled next to me and helped himself to the other two joints like they were Halloween candy.

"You a beaner?" Brad frowned.

I didn't know what a beaner was, but judging from the look on his face, it couldn't be good. There was a moment of silence. I had a sense of impending danger. They had me and they knew it.

Lord Ricky stood up, so I stood up, too. I'd get no sympathy from these guys if they thought I would mess up the balance of their beach. Lord Ricky handed me my bag and felt me up a bit. He dug his face into my neck and sniffed me.

"She doesn't smell like a beaner," he said.

"But Nuevo, that's Mexican," Brad sniggered.

"No," I said. "It's Hawaiian, N-u-u-h-i-w-a, like David."

Brad's mouth dropped, and Lord Ricky's eyes opened wide. Suddenly they were crazed. Sounds, not words, tumbled out of their mouths. All together they were saying things like, "Ya. Jah. Foth."

The way they were twisting around made them look like they were high on *Guiana*—that's a drug made from frog slime. My dad told me he'd seen people trip on that stuff for days at a time.

Lord Ricky waltzed with me cheek to cheek. Brad and Stu swooned next to him and hummed. Then Lord Ricky said, "David Nuuhiwa, alright."

Uh-oh. I had just wanted to tell them how to say my name. I didn't mean to give them the impression that David Nuuhiwa, the badass surfer from Hawaii, was related to me. But it was too late. Lord Ricky was giving me the *shaka* cool sign, pinkie and thumb raised, wrist shaking back and forth. Brad and Stu backed up just far enough for me to break free.

"Well, goodbye," I said.

Brad and Stu crossed their arms, tucking their palms under their armpits, nodding, and said, "Alright, Nani Nuuhiwa. Alright."

I had done it. I had gotten past the gargoyles and I was looking good. I flipped my hair to one side and reached out to say goodbye to Lord Ricky. I touched the dog tags around his neck and saw the name Ray Stevens on them. Still holding them in my hand I asked, "Wow. Mary Jo's brother?"

It took less than a second to realize I had made a terrible mistake. Lord Ricky grabbed the bandana around my neck. Spit sprayed all over my face as he pulled me in closer and asked, "Do you know what the ultimate sacrifice is?"

As a matter of fact, I did. It was when a soldier died for his country. I realized that's how Mary Jo got into the lineup. Ray must have eaten it in 'Nam so the lineup gave her a mercy pass. Lord Ricky pulled the scarf tighter. I started to choke. He was so angry that his face went purple.

"Have you ever ID'd body parts after they were in an airtight coffin for a week? Half a body stuffed into a uniform with hair and teeth attached to something that looked like your best friend's face. Have you? Ever hold the American flag after it was folded by an honor guard? You ever do anything like that?"

I shook my head.

How could I have blown it so bad? I wanted to cry but that would have been uncool.

The men at the volleyball court stopped playing and looked our way. Brad stepped behind me, trying to block their view. Lord Ricky grabbed my bandana even tighter until we were nose to nose and I was on my tippy toes. Stu pointed to my bandana trying to come between me and Lord Ricky as he said, "Rick, look what you're holding onto, man. Air Cav. See. 'Have guns. Will travel.'"

Talk about a talisman. On the patch, just below the skull with wings, were the words, AIR CAV WARRIOR SPIRIT. Seeing that design brought Lord Ricky back to reality and saved my life. He gently put me down and patted the top of my head.

"You got friends in the Air Cavalry?" he asked.

I could breathe again. "Yes, lots of them," I said.

Stu was waving and smiling at the men on the volleyball court, trying to get everybody focused on the game again, but they weren't buying it. He was like a ventriloquist when he told me, "Nani, be a good girl and wave to the guys about to kick our asses."

Because I wanted to cry, I thought about the *Ed Sullivan Show* and Señor Wences, the little painted hand puppet I loved so much. I did what Stu told me to do and waved.

"I really miss Ray, ya know?" Lord Ricky said.

He took my hair into his hands and held it like a blanket. Then he blew his nose and wiped his face in it. I centered myself before asking, "Can I go meet Mary Jo now?"

He looked at me for a moment, released my hair, sat back down on the garbage can, and signaled me forward.

I hurried down the beach toward the lineup. They were still facing the water, completely unaware of what had happened behind them.

CHAPTER TWELVE

Initiation II: Fish Empress

At the green wall where all the gay guys sat, it was another party day at State. A radio was blasting a high-pitched soprano singing some weird German song. Men with mustaches were eating crustless sandwiches and drinking wine from the bottle.

The gays were on my left. Each was more beautiful than the next. They sat close together for protection like schools of fish. Oiled to the gills, most of them were smoking and soaking up every ounce of sun their bronzed bodies could absorb.

A little farther down the beach, almost to the water, I walked past some girls who were playing with a cootie catcher. Their fingers were under paper flaps that looked like a flower opening and closing. The air stunk of patchouli and clove cigarettes mixed with cherry incense burning on clumps of sand. This had to be the Topanga clique. They wore off-the-shoulder peasant dresses, see-through ponchos, and patched denim bikinis.

As they played, one of the girls moved her index fingers and thumbs in and out, side to side, and asked, "Will the McBride twins be here today?"

She flipped open one of the inner triangles and read the answer, "Definitely not."

In unison all the girls sighed and went back to eating avocado and sprouts sandwiches on wheat berry bread and talking about having a bad case of the munchies.

The lineup sat in front of the Topanga Girls covering their noses with the corners of their towels as incense blew in their faces. I reminded myself not to look too self-confident. I made a mental note of each girl's strategic placement in the lineup. Their positions defined their power at State. In the center, of course, were Rox and Claire. The Lisas sat to Claire's right. KC, the girl with a shag haircut, sat on the end. She wore Arnold Palmer Ray-Bans, a knit bikini with a zigzag pattern, and had tube sock tan lines. On the other side of Rox, two perfect mannequin types sat side by side. That had to be Suzie in the crochet cream and powder blue bathing suit with the perfect part down the middle of her hair. And Jenni wore a bikini with a strapless top. She was so sweetly beautiful with her beaded Indian purse and matching barrettes. Next to them at the far end was Mary Jo's spot. Her towel was there, but she was nowhere in sight. *Where was she?* I came to a grinding halt.

"Fight!" somebody yelled.

I turned around and saw a kid in an open aloha shirt and trunks sagging halfway off his butt kicking sand in the face of a guy who looked like Tarzan.

"Faggot!" he yelled at the top of his lungs.

Another boy standing next to him was lighting matches and tossing them at the man's friend, who was lying on his belly looking up at him. The boy was saying, "I hate you, I hate you, and I hate you." Then he lit the whole matchbook and dropped it.

From behind me, I heard Claire say to Rox, "They're gonna get beat up again. You better do something."

Rox stood and turned toward the action at the same time that I turned around toward her. We both walked forward and did the full-on frontal smash. Worst of all, it was 100 percent my fault. I should have jumped out of the way, but I was too starstruck so our foreheads collided.

"Wipe out," a lifeguard said laughing as he ran up the beach to break up the crowd.

"What's your problem?" Rox snapped at me as she pushed her tortoiseshell shades up into her hair. She had sky blue eyes, high cheekbones, and a perfect little beauty mark on her cheek. She reeked of Bain de Soleil.

"Sorry," I said.

I smiled and tried to look happy.

"Is Mary Jo around?"

Thank God the Valium had kicked in. The lineup looked like a firing squad ready to carry out any order Rox gave them.

"No," she said and pushed past me.

The lineup rushed after her, except Claire. She lingered, mulling me over, assessing every detail about my hair, my halter top, and my flip-flops. She didn't talk. She just looked long and hard. Slowly circling, she sucked on a lollipop and twirled a dangling turquoise earring. Her eyes were hypnotic.

I felt like I was spinning. I had never seen that color aqua before. They matched her turquoise perfectly.

"You wanna go out?" she asked, pointing to the waves.

Just my luck, the no surfing blackball flag was flying. State was going off with a six-foot break and there was no place to run. I had to go for it.

"Can I leave my stuff here?" I asked.

"Of course," Claire said, all friendly.

Believe it or not, all I could think of was the 23rd Psalm: *Yea, though I walk through the valley of the shadow of death, I will fear no evil; for Thou art with me; Thy rod and Thy staff they comfort me.* I hated the way Jean's Catholic voodoo came into my mind when I was scared.

Claire watched me take everything off except the rabbit foot tethered to my bikini and the scarf around my neck.

Rox looked back over her shoulder at us. She was still pissed off but when she caught Claire's eye, her frown turned into a grin. There was no time to translate what that meant. Claire didn't move, so I realized that I was supposed to lead the way. My hands were shaking. I had never been in surf this big before without a board, but I had to act cool, and I did. Luckily, no one was paying attention to us. That's the way it is at the beach. No one cares about chick stuff.

I waded out to my knees. This was not *my* Pacific Ocean. It was dark, thick with kelp, and so cold it stung. I let my palms float on top of the swirling whitewash. I spread my fingers to pay homage to *Ae Kai*, the place where land and sea meet. The water was splashing hard against me. I turned my back to the waves. Claire sashayed right past me. I had never seen a *haole* girl edge out toward the break like that. *Some girls*, I thought, *just belong to the water.* Obviously she was a Pisces.

A path of suntan oil glistened behind Claire, which made it easy for me to follow her over the ditches and jagged rocks that made State so dangerous. Everything was cool until the ocean got so deep that I couldn't bounce off the bottom to keep my head out of the water. What the hell was I going to do? Panicking only made things worse. I needed to relax and let the power of the sea lift me up and carry me out.

Claire kicked hard and dove under the first wave. Six-footers slammed overhead, pushing me down and tossing me around like a rag doll. I popped up, filled my lungs with air and got ready for the next wall of water. Body surfing is an event that you have to do alone. Claire and I knew that calling for help was not an option. And besides, she had given me a dare and I had accepted. Now it was time to put up or shut up. Once I realized that, the rest was simple. Catching the current was like flying under water. The bigger the wave, the deeper I dove and the calmer the ocean seemed.

When there are really big waves, the only survival technique is to dive under the turbulence as far as you can and wait for the sunlight to appear above you and then paddle toward it. Underwater, my eyes strained looking for swarms of tiny jellyfish that hung like miniature chandeliers beneath the surface. When I rose up, I stretched my arms high over my head and kicked as hard as I could to stay above water as long as possible.

Dropping down the spine of a giant wave, I saw Claire floating on her back outside the breakers. She looked totally peaceful and at one with the sea. As a bunch of pelicans flew over us in a V-shaped formation, a thought raced through my mind. *If I could be friends with Claire, all my problems would vanish.*

I couldn't take my eyes off her long white hair, which was making a halo of light around her face. She was cosmic, singing a Loggins & Messina song.

"Is that 'Vahevala?'" I asked, paddling over.

She didn't answer. The only sound was the ocean splashing up against my face. I wanted to say something but the rule was I had to wait until she spoke to me. Circling around silently, I understood the power of Claire. On the beach she seemed frail, but in the water she was strong. It was usually that way with beach chicks. Aquatic strength was another key to power. Surfers didn't like wimpy girls, and they didn't like jocks either. They liked girls who looked like mermaids in the water. Annie taught me that the ideal girl had a combination of beauty and strength like Claire did. Rolling up with the swell gave me the perspective I needed. I now understood that Claire guarded the gate of liquid cool at State, and Rox ruled the sand.

From the vantage point of the take-off zone, I realized two more things. One: a surfboard would make it easier for me to scope out who was onshore. Two: seeing the lineup on the beach made it clear what their role was. Without them, surfers wouldn't have anybody to witness what they did. It was up to the girls to make sure each wave, and the surfer on it, was remembered. They were like historians or something.

Up close, I could see Claire's ears were underwater. She hadn't heard a word I said. But something didn't look right. Her brow was furrowed and the muscles in her face were so tight that her neck veins pulsed. She was struggling to get her wind back. I could see she was in trouble but it was best not to say anything. Annie taught me that letting a local keep face was more important than asking if they were okay.

"What grade are you in?" she said, barely getting the words out without swallowing water.

"Tenth in September," I told her.

We dog paddled next to each other. Our toes touched accidently.

"You going to Pali High?" she asked.

Before I could say yes, Claire's face disappeared below the waterline. When she resurfaced, she was red as a pomegranate and gasping for air. My initiation was over.

When someone is drowning, they cling to anything or anyone close by. Because of that, sometimes both people end up drowning. With my mind racing in a hundred different directions, I kicked away from Claire. She grabbed at the water, trying to reach me, and then her head went completely under.

There was no time to figure out the cool thing to do so I did what my dad taught me. I dove way underneath Claire and grabbed her from behind. That way she wouldn't be able to panic and pull me down. Under the water, my right arm grazed her ribs and locked over her chest. I flipped her body away from mine. At the same time, I used my left hand to push into her lower back to float her face up to the surface.

She was limp as I paddled away from the take-off zone. Her broad shoulders and narrow hips made her easy to maneuver in the water. After about fifteen minutes of dog paddling, Claire was still floating in front of me. I finally asked, "How are you doing?"

Claire slowly stretched her arms wide as if waking from a deep sleep and smiled. She said, "I'm fine," in a sassy sing-song voice.

She was laughing and breathing easy. I jerked away, realizing I had been had.

"I peed on you," she said and spit a mouthful of water at me. "Did you feel it?"

Half of me sank right there in the ocean.

"I was telling you in my own special way to piss off." She laughed again and waved at the lineup. All the girls were standing up watching, laughing, and waving back.

"Now I'm going to make sure you never bother us again."

Claire snatched at my bathing suit top but missed it by inches. Then she laid back and kicked water in my face. My eyes stung. I couldn't see her but I felt something moving down my legs as she grabbed my bathing suit bottom and pulled it to my knees. She would have gotten it totally off but I kicked her in the head, pulled them back up, and paddled for the first wave I could get. She swam after me and yelled, "Don't ever come back to State, dorkus!"

I figured she'd probably get her wish because the wave I was about to take was most likely going to kill me anyway.

The swell had picked up to at least eight feet with a ten-foot drop. It was a total close out. I didn't care. I had blown it big time. I was ready to die, and I didn't care if it hurt.

Flying over the lip of the giant wave on my belly was like seeing God, getting totally off, and then paying for all the sins of mankind. I got myself tubed, but without the speed of a board, the wave closed in and ate me alive. I bounced off the ocean floor, pounded by the whitewash. The only thing that gave me satisfaction was knowing Claire would eat it next.

Adjusting my top, I watched Claire stretch out her arm and power into a huge wave. She dropped out of it ahead of the break. It was like watching someone go over Niagara Falls without a barrel. All I could see were her feet curling into a crackling vat of whitewater. She must have gone head-first into the rocks. She got exactly what she deserved.

Lord Ricky saluted me as I plowed through the white-wash toward the beach. He was lying by his board next to Brad and Stu. There were about twelve blonde guys in front of them waxing their boards, perched and ready to surf.

"Hurry up!" one of them yelled.

I couldn't tell if he was yelling at me or to the lifeguard slowly lowering the no surf flag. Why couldn't I just die already? Behind me, Claire was acting all dramatic and stuff. She was coughing and splashing all around. All I could think about was getting away from State and hiding at 33 Sage until school started in September.

I hurried out of the water, face lowered and tongue push-ing against the roof of my mouth so I wouldn't cry. I turned to take one last look at the ocean. Claire was bobbing up and down as another wave crashed over her.

"Aren't ya gonna help ya friend?" Lord Ricky asked.

Jean always told me, "Once a mistake, twice a fool." There was no way I was risking my life for that bitch. Did she really think I was so stupid that I'd fall for that drowning act again? Hell, even the lineup wasn't interested in Act II. Rox was busy chatting with some major babes and didn't even bother to look up.

Lord Ricky was waiting. If I wanted to get off the beach in one piece, I had to do what he said. I gave him a thumbs up and pushed my way back into the water. Claire was acting all corpse-like, floating facedown with her arms spread wide. I tied a doubled knot into my suit top before I reached for her. I pulled her up by her hair. I looked at her face. Her eyes were not focused. She didn't even put up a fight or say anything mean. I turned her over and put my hand up to her mouth feeling for air. Her front teeth were chipped in half and when I pushed my fist hard into her stomach, water and barf came out. It wasn't an act this time.

Claire pleaded with me, "Don't let anyone see me," and barfed again.

She hung onto my arm as the throw up floated past us. I wanted to let her wash up on shore like the shipwreck she was, but I couldn't. She lay in my arms with her nipple poking out of her top. Sure, she was a world-class bitch, but she was in trouble. Still, I had certain conditions.

"Say I'm not a dork," I insisted.

Claire couldn't stand. I held her until she looked up at me and slowly said, "You are not a dork."

"I gotta fix your top."

"Hurry," she answered.

I didn't. My hands and her body were underwater. No one could see me move my fingers slowly over her nipple, tucking the cloth over her breast.

"Am I in?" she asked.

"Sort of." I waved at Lord Ricky and told Claire that he was watching.

She closed her eyes and struggled to breathe. Claire needed me. We both knew it. What a great way to get thrown off the beach, carrying my executioner back to the chopping block. What planet was I on?

Just then I remembered the rule about not outshining the main girls on their own turf. I looked at Claire long and hard. Then I gently smoothed her hair back over her head and helped her to her feet. She wasn't even paying attention.

"Oh no," she mumbled, "It's Bob."

It made me happy to see her bummed out with sand grinding between what was left of her teeth. Bob was a lifeguard and clearly a regular fixture at State. He looked like a lumberjack with his huge barrel chest, baseball bat–like arms, long stride, and jet-black hair. He came toward us with a red buoy over his shoulder, looking official. When Bob jogged past the surfers, they all booed. Bob ignored them.

"Pretend you like me," I told Claire.

By the time he reached us, Claire and I were arm in arm. Claire smiled and put her head on my shoulder. Even with a mouth full of busted teeth and barf breath, she was still totally hot. Trying to trudge out of the water, she wobbled like a drunk and tripped face-first into a ditch. I picked her up and let the fast-flowing tide push us forward. We sat down below the sand drift, using it to shield us from the locals' radar.

Bob stood in front of us looking pissed off. He didn't notice what a mess she was. He was too busy chewing her out for being stupid enough to go into such rough surf.

"That was your last drowning," he said.

"No problem, Bob," Claire said without opening her mouth or moving her lips.

Even then, under the most extreme circumstances, she could act totally cool. Her bikini looked glued onto her rock-hard body. Her out-of-focus eyes were beautiful. To me, she was still the star of State and the queen of *Haolewood*.

"That was quite a save," Bob told me.

Looking down at Claire, he pointed at me and said, "You should be nice to her."

I wondered if his words meant anything to Claire.

She nodded and slipped her hand into mine. I knew she wasn't for real but it felt good to feel her trembling fingers. Claire hated me. But if she'd just like me for the rest of the afternoon, I would die happy.

"What's your name, Five-O?" Bob asked me.

Why did everyone get off on that television show? It must have been the wave in the opening credits or something.

"Nani," I said, smiling.

"That means 'beautiful' in Hawaiian, right?" Bob asked. My jaw almost dropped off my face. "Surprised you, didn't I?"

He continued and shifted the buoy from one shoulder to the other, exposing the black hair in his armpits.

"Well, if the bikini fits . . ." Bob said, thinking he was funny.

I wondered if I was supposed to say something but before I could, Bob said, "wear it," finishing his own sentence.

Bob was one of the reasons beach people had a reputation for being stupid. He strolled back to his station tower, pointed his finger at us like a gun, and shot. Then he blew the smoke from the muzzle and slipped it in into his imaginary holster.

"'Book 'em.' Aloha," he said.

The locals booed him again as he passed in front of them and Bob ignored them.

I stuck my finger down my throat. Claire smiled.

"Claire, isn't your dad a dentist?" Bob shouted, turning back to us one more time.

"He's an ophthalmologist, you dweeb," Claire said. As she spoke, little flecks of bloody spit sprayed onto my arms.

"Sorry," she groaned, putting her head down on her knees.

I couldn't help but wonder if she was sorry for spitting blood on me or if she was sorry for being a royal pain in the ass. Obviously I would never say the "c word," but honestly, I couldn't find a better one to describe her. She was looking more like a rebel Gemini and less like a Pisces every minute.

Claire pointed to my knee.

"Oh no," I said.

My knee looked like it had gotten its period. Clumps of thick blood trickled down the side of my leg. It was hard for me to imagine how something that looked that scary hadn't hurt enough for me to notice.

"Is it bad?" Claire asked. Of course it's bad, I wanted to say. Just open your eyes. But then I realized she wasn't asking about me. She wanted to know about her teeth.

"You look like Red Skelton," I told her. I didn't have to remind Claire what a freak he was, in his clown costume with blackout gum across his front teeth.

We sat for another moment in silence. Then Claire did something extraordinary. She reached over and gently pulled a blade of sea grass from my bleeding knee and threw it to the side. That tiny gesture changed my world.

Bob was hoisting the surfing flag. We were in the stampede zone. If we didn't move quickly, at least one of us would get run over. Claire raised her index finger like she was summoning a waiter at a fancy restaurant.

"Can you walk on that mess?" she asked.

"If you can talk, I can walk," I said.

What a great line. But it was not so easy to get up or extend my hand to Claire. Before we both stood, Rox was standing over us, jaw tight, tilting her head.

"What's going on here?" she asked, her hands on her hips. Then she did the eerie stare thing with her eyes. Mary Jo called it freezing. That's when she stopped blinking and twisted her lips into a tight little grin. I felt tongue-tied looking up at her. Then Claire broke out in a big smile.

"Holy crap. What happened to you?" Rox asked.

She helped Claire stand up and said, "Now you and Shawn really do make the perfect couple. Neither one of you have all your front teeth."

"Shhh. That's a secret," Claire said.

I watched them walk back to their towels.

Of course Rox and Claire wouldn't let me in the lineup. What the hell was I thinking? Guys ran past me into the water. I had to dodge their surfboards and look casual at the same time. I strolled up the beach trying to figure out how to get my stuff and how long it would take me to swim home to Hawaii. When I heard someone whistle, I turned around and saw Claire and Rox.

"Are you coming or not?" Rox barked.

She stood there, arms folded tight across her chest, pushing her giant boobs up under her chin. That's when it hit me. Rox was waiting for me. This meant only one thing for sure: the initiation had just begun.

CHAPTER THIRTEEN

Secrets

The lineup was like a surf intelligentsia. They questioned me about everything. But there were five secrets they'd never get out of me. These five things I would go to the grave with before I told anyone, especially the lineup:

1. All the stuff about stealing my dad's ashes.

2. I'm afraid of the dark. I wake up every single night at 3:10 a.m. It has been that way ever since Dad's heart attack. There was nothing I could do to keep from waking up. I had the creeps, that's what I called it. It was like a switch went off in my head in the middle of the night. A memory grabbed me and took me to spooky places. Sounds came from everywhere in the dark and held me down. I thought of vampires, ghosts, and snakes. There weren't any snakes on Hawaii. In fact, I have never seen a real snake, but I was still terrified at 3:10 a.m.

I was too scared to move. I was a prisoner in my own bed. I just wanted to suck my thumb or rock back and forth until someone came down the hall to comfort me.

Since Jean went back to nursing, her shifts were often from seven at night to seven in the morning. The creeps were the worst when Jean wasn't home. I actually missed hearing her snore like a storm off Hilo in the winter. She snored so loudly that I imagined the sound knocking small birds out of the sky to their deaths. Regardless of whether Jean was home, it was Dad who used to stay with me until I fell asleep. I hugged Mrs. Beasley and watched the shadows on my walls.

Now when I worried, nobody came. And it didn't matter. I was almost sixteen for Christ's sake. I didn't need someone to put a cool towel on my forehead or tell me I was loved. Three ten in the morning belonged to me and the ocean. With no street traffic, I could hear the waves at State crashing. Their rhythm relaxed me just the way Dad's voice used to do. If I woke up from a bad dream, he'd tell me, "No worries."

3. I totally eavesdropped on the lineup to get State wired. This might not sound like a big deal, but it is. If I blew their trust, I blew it all. I was careful. I sat quietly next to Mary Jo with my eyes closed. The lineup relaxed around me. They were chatty and impressed that I had survived Claire's cannibalistic charm. I acted more like a rescued pet in need of companionship than the newest member of the Bod Squad. In my mind, I filed away each of their secrets, knowing it would help me maintain my spot among them.

Lisa Yates was the intense party girl with a voice that sounded as if she'd smoked fifty packs of cigarettes a day. When she talked, her lips pressed forward as if they had gotten stuck halfway through a kiss. She always wore Indian print bikinis. Lisa had OD'd on baby aspirin in the third grade because she thought they were candy and almost blew herself up with fireworks in the fourth. No one knew she had permanent eye damage but refused to wear glasses. That's why she was always arm-in-arm with the other Lisa and sometimes looked klutzy. She was a Capricorn and had the best sense of humor in the lineup.

Lisa Haskell, on the other hand, was a Sagittarius. She was spontaneous and hated rules. She was always scheming ways to get cigarettes and knew every bit of gossip from State to Malibu. Lisa Haskell was a Mormon and coveted her autographed copy of the Osmond Brothers' *Hello* album. One of her brothers went on his mission in Las Vegas and met all the Osmonds. Lisa H.'s biggest secret was that she had to leave her house wearing a Jantzen one-piece with a modesty panel. She changed when she got to State into her ridiculously small checked bikini. No one knew this but the Lisas and me.

Suzie Quinn was being groomed to rule State after Rox graduated. She looked like a stick of gold with thinly plucked eyebrows and super wavy long hair. Suzie was not thrilled about hosting a new girl, but she was glad Rox snapped me up before the Topangas got their dibs on me. Suzie's biggest secret was that she had broken a major rule by going all the way with a surf god at State before she was officially his girlfriend. She was planning on going all the way with him again before the summer was over. But she refused to name the guy. Suzie was an Aries like Uncle Mike, charming, determined, very ambitious, and quick-tempered.

Jenni (with an "i" not "y" or "ie") Fox was Suzie's best friend. Jenni was beyond beautiful. Guys called her Jen or Fox and loved her because she was super shy and blushed when they talked to her. Jenni never bickered with anyone and was always in a good mood. Even Rox loved her. Jenni was graceful, willowy, and always talked in a soft voice. No one thought she ever got angry, but I learned that if she had the hiccups, it meant she was pissed off. Jenni was a Libra. For her it was all about looking patient, calm, and most importantly fair to everyone. She was the nicest to me, and I loved her violet bikinis and Yardley Eau de London perfume. It was like sitting next to a field of clover and jasmine. But what impressed me most about Jenni was that she thought about her future. She was going to become a stewardess and live in Paris.

KC Smith was a tomboy and the dark cloud in the group. She always wore tight-knit bikinis and was an Aquarius, which is a notoriously difficult persona. She had broad butterfly shoulders, a tiny waist, no hips, long legs, and a flat chest. She had been banished to the far side of the lineup after she cut all the highlights out of her long blonde hair into a shoulder-length shag. Now it was too dark to be called blonde. Rox was barely talking to her. I think if KC weren't captain of the Pali High volleyball team, she would have been out altogether. Cutting her hair was a big mistake. It reminded me that a lot of rules are worth saying again and again:

Never cut your hair.

That first week at State, the waves were small and summer school had started. It was no secret that surfers weren't into

IQ status and most of them ended up repeating a class or two. We had the beach to ourselves until noon. The silence reminded me of military maneuvers on Pearl Harbor Day. Those peach-fuzzed sailors would stand absolutely still in the noontime sun while ceremonies on the USS *Arizona* dragged on and on. They were stiff as statues dressed in white cotton pants that flapped in the wind. With their arms tight behind their backs and chins raised, the sun scorched them like burnt Wonder Bread.

At times during the day, I sunk so low and lay so still in the sand I felt invisible. Claire and Rox would talk like I wasn't there. Of course, Rox and Claire were the most interesting to listen to. They were stoked because their boyfriends, Jerry and Shawn, were finally coming back from surfing down in Ensenada. The main order of business was to get seriously tan. That took concentration. Two hours on the front, two hours on the back, tops untied, until they were well roasted.

Here's what I saw during the tanning time: Rox checked her tampon string when she rolled to her left. Claire rubbed Sun-In on her treasure trail to keep the thin hairs between her belly button and bikini white. Claire also needed help retying her top, and if she fell asleep sitting up, she had a tendency to leave her mouth wide open. Rox, on the other hand, never slept; she was like a hawk waiting for something weak and easy to tear apart. I learned both Claire and Rox carried nail scissors in their bags to clip roving pubic hairs that snuck out of their suits, and they checked each other's teeth for leftover food, even though I never saw them eat. Seriously, Rox never ate.

Rox was also so terrified of bees, she'd hide under her towel if she heard anything buzzing. Claire called it melissophobia. That word would have really impressed Miss Meli once upon a time. The lineup's number one job was to be Rox's lookout. No bee ever came within ten feet of us.

Claire would brush Rox's hair as she chatted on about the spider veins in her mother's nose, her fear of getting pockmarks from pimples, and her total hatred of the paddle tennis tournaments she was forced to play at the Bel-Air Bay Club. Claire also hated her house on San Remo Drive. She hated the fake geraniums in terra-cotta planters outside the front door and her little brother's oversized iguana tank that made the hall to her room smell like fish food.

I found it amusing that Claire had a Steiff puppet collection in her bedroom and mounted them on Coke bottles to show off her favorites. Hansi the parakeet, Gatty the gator, and Cocki the puppy were above her bed, but the love of her life, after Shawn McBride, was Jacko the monkey. She loved Jacko so much that she carried him in her purse. To protect him from the sand, she wrapped him in Saran wrap so he had his own little wet suit. That was her big secret, before her new teeth.

Rox acted like a member of the Russian Intelligence or KGB; she spoke softly and never talked if someone was standing too close. Her perfect white teeth rarely showed because Rox never smiled. And she never ever spoke about her parents' deaths. I learned about the car crash from listening to the Lisas.

"Here today," Lisa H. said.

"Gone tomorrow," said Lisa Y.

I knew what that was all about because it was the same for my dad. One minute he was on his way to work to open the bar and have a beer, the next minute he was lying on the ground, in a coma before they even got him to the hospital.

Rox never shed a tear about her parents dying, but she sobbed endlessly when Jerry Richmond dumped her after their first hot date, which left a permanent stain on her sister's new couch. That was the start of their on-and-off romance. Right now it was on, but when it was off, Rox cried, and when she cried she looked like a heaving sack of bones.

She said their last breakup happened because Jerry was a horny Taurus. That made me gag because my dad was a Taurus, too. I thought of Taurus men as hard-headed, consistent types, not sex fiends.

The tone of Rox's voice totally changed when she described getting back together with Jerry and her first time in the fort. She said Jerry's skin felt like velvet.

"Yeah. The fort," said Claire, "that castle in the sky. The best place in the world."

The fort was a secret hideaway at Claire's boyfriend's house. It was off-limits to everyone except Claire, Rox, and Jerry.

The weirdest thing about Rox and Claire was their relationship to the ocean. It accounts for almost two-thirds of the earth's surface and was crashing right in front of them, but they only seemed to notice it when guys were surfing. The Pacific with all its unseen truth was like wallpaper to them, and the sound of waves seemed no more important than the hum of an air conditioner in their biology class. I don't think they even realized there were fish and a whole lot of other living things out there. It was obvious that neither of them had ever been on a board. It was a prime rule:

GIRLS DON'T SURF.

That rule really bugged me, but I wasn't about to say anything, and I sure as hell wasn't going to tell them that I surfed Waikiki when I was little. I remembered what Annie Iopa told me about what happened to girls who were stupid enough to surf.

4. The fact that I knew how to surf was my fourth biggest secret. It was another one I would take to the grave.

Every day it was the same, that first week in the lineup. I'd pretend to wake up and uncoil my hair from around my face. Claire thought I was cute, but Rox wasn't sure. I could tell by the way she looked at me when I rolled over, retied my top and lit up. The Lisas, Jenni, and even Suzie talked to me. But Rox just watched and listened.

The other lineup member who barely gave me the time of day was Mary Jo. She was furious about missing my initiation. Seems she went looking for me. I don't know how we didn't see each other, but making a Leo feel unappreciated was the worst thing I could have done. No matter what I told her, no matter how many times I apologized, she was still ticked off.

At the end of the day, I didn't get anything like a quick kiss goodbye from Rox but I did occasionally get a nod.

That was always a relief. I was sitting at State Beach by the lineup. I knew exactly what I needed to do next: keep my eyes low, continue to be selective when I spoke, collect the cigarette butts I smoked and zip them up in a baggie, walk home for another meatloaf dinner, and figure out how to get Rox to like me.

5. I like looking at pictures of naked women. I started reading *Playboy* in my Uncle Mike's guest bathroom when I was eight. Uncle Mike never used the guest suite on his estate. It had a giant bedroom with cashmere blankets everywhere and a zebra skin rug that lay under a pair of vinyl-ribbed chairs that were fun to spin around on. The bathroom had an oversized Jacuzzi tub for Japanese investors and all of his friends who were getting divorced. There were scented soaps and flat edge razors and white seal hairbrushes. Every month the new issue of *Playboy* was added to the big stack he kept in that woven rattan basket next to the toilet. Stealing centerfolds from the magazines might not have been the smartest thing to do, but there was no time to second-guess myself before I left. It's not like I could walk into State Liquor and buy one. What would I say?

"Hi, I'm fifteen. Can I have the newest issue of *Playboy*, please?"

I took the December 1971 magazine with my favorite centerfold from his special rattan basket. I stuck it in a *Cosmopolitan* that had Lauren Hutton on the cover. No one on the planet could ever know I liked *Playboy*. I would even tell myself that I just liked the dirty cartoons, Little Annie Fanny, Joe Namath's Pub Cologne ads, and the Vargas paintings of girls in garter belts and top hats. Sometimes I'd even pretend to read one of the long interviews with people like Roman Polanski or Francesco Scavullo. Like most guys out there, I whipped through the *Field and Stream* pages and past the giant Remington Shaver ad to get to the centerfold.

I had the same fantasy every time. Michelle Porter, a.k.a. Miss December, was from Wisconsin. I loved her wavy blonde hair and long eyelashes that were painted on the picture with a crow quill pen. The way they were done gave her eyes a come-get-me look. I never got enough of the way Miss December posed for the camera.

I really liked the white *haole* girls. There was just something about a girl who hid from the sun that got me going. Just like Miss December, the other centerfolds were perfect, all airbrushed and smooth. They looked edible, like peach lollipops.

Afterward, I'd lay still, peaceful and sleepy. Thinking of nothing. The nirvana lasted just a few minutes and then the pictures seemed creepy, and the topless women seemed like dangerous informants, spies and blackmailers who would tell everyone I was a *Funny Kine* girl. I'd die if that ever happened. My lust turned into paranoia, and I crawled away from them sideways like a crab. I quickly shoved the centerfolds into their hiding spot inside the *Cosmo* cover, put my flannel nightgown back on, washed my hands, and ran to my room. As fast as I could, I opened my sleeping bag and stuck the magazine inside next to the pickle jar of my dad's stash. I looked every which way to make sure no one was watching even though I was alone. I tossed everything quickly to the top shelf of my closet and promised myself I'd never look at a *Playboy* again.

CHAPTER FOURTEEN

t-surfers rule

I hated Jean more than Hitler.

The taste of last night's dinner—ham salad with gherkins and mayo—moved from my stomach up to my mouth. It was stupid of me to try to be like Dad and actually drink the Daddy-tini this morning. For some weird reason, I thought it would bring him closer. Drop the wall that separates the living from the dead and make it possible for me to feel him close. I should have known better than to actually swallow let alone gulp the whole thing down. I had to hold my nose. The vodka burned my throat. It was so hot. Not like frying pan grease, but like liquid horseradish. Like Agent Orange torching an explosive reaction deep in my gut. When I drank it, I imagined my dad standing in our old kitchen giving me a thumbs up.

I was drunk. Somehow I made it to State, plopped myself against the wall outside the volleyball courts, and smoked half a pack of Larks before dawn. My legs wobbled when I tried to stand, making me think the mixture of vodka and orange juice for breakfast wasn't such a good idea.

Any minute I was going to throw up. It was tearing apart my innards. How did Daddy drink this stuff every morning? Maybe I should have added some papaya or ginger. Maybe the protein powder and wheat germ made it easier to keep down. What was I thinking?

I almost didn't have enough time to stick my hand over my mouth and make it to the bathroom. There must have been a rule:

Never barf in public.

The only person who saw me was Lōlō. He and his scary dog were on the empty beach, roving from garbage can to garbage can, gnawing on tiny chicken bones. They watched me curiously as I ran past them, tying my hair up in a knot. A big whiff of Lōlō's wet cardboard shoes and mildewed clothes was all it took for the barf to come up my throat. I could picture myself choking up Jean's cooking all over the beach. I was in big trouble. The dog growled and looked like he was going to bite me. But that didn't stop me from running.

Beach bathrooms were hot spots for trouble. No one ever went in alone. But I had no time to check for freaks. There wasn't even a second to adjust to the stink of the place before I lunged forward, slammed my knees on the cold, wet pavement, and stuck my head in a toilet with someone else's piss in it.

With my head in the porcelain bowl, I prayed to a god my father said didn't exist. I puked out a nasty stream of Jean's salad mixed with the entire mug of Daddy-tini.

"Help me, Jesus," I said as I puked again and again.

The churchwomen on the big island would secretly pray to Pele. They said Madame Pele was so strong and mighty she could snap the world in two. But all I could think of was Jean's little white Jesus and the words *Deo Favente*. I didn't understand what that meant, all I knew was it was Catholic talk and I needed all the help I could get. I hated the way Jean's church filled my brain with a stained-glass god, crucified in red, but I kept saying those two words anyway, over and over again, praying for some kind of divine intervention.

My mother's god liked it when you kneeled and prayed. I figured it was a good time to repent since I was already down there. I said, "I'm sorry, Jesus. I went to second base with Ben Keameka, and I stole his sister's double strand puka shell necklace. I'm sorry I broke Mr. Iokepa's ukulele and blamed it on Vickie Tanaka. I'm sorry I called Vickie a Daikon Fatty Leg Girl and told everyone in the third grade she ate her boogers." Every jolt and heave made me pant and bend lower. I looked down at my purse and saw the Band-Aid box at the bottom.

"And I'm sorry Jesus, once and for all, I faked out Jean and took my dad's ashes. I'm sorry for everything."

I held onto a rusted pipe and waited for the next wave to hit me. I waited a minute but nothing happened so I leaned my head against the stall door and slowly stood. I had to get out of there. I balanced myself and stepped over the garbage that covered the cement floor: a comb, half a cockroach lying belly up, and a ripped Jack of Diamonds. My eyes had adjusted to the darkness. All around me, on every wall, the words ⸸-SURFERS RULE were written in bold, black letters. The felt-tip graffiti made me sway from side to side as a light bulb flickered on and off. I examined each cinderblock, wondering who "⸸-surfers" were.

Everything was spinning 'round and 'round. Thinking made my head feel like it was one of the pegs in the ring toss on King Kamehameha Day. That was my favorite holiday. But before I could start thinking about Hilo Hattie, who I loved, and the Tapa Room's fruit-packed Shirley Temples, I heard some girls coming.

I stumbled toward the sink and checked my face in the cracked mirror to make sure that nothing disgusting was stuck to it. No matter who was coming in, they could never connect me to the mess I left in the second stall. I slammed a Fireball jawbreaker into my mouth and let my hair down. Filaments of dust were caught in the light. It was officially morning.

I leaned over the sink and watched through my hair as four girls entered, offering broad, toothy smiles as if to say "we bite." Hopefully I'd be nothing to them but a blur in the corner. I knew they weren't locals. They were chewing bubble gum and cracking it on their back teeth. They had frosted white lips, blue mascara, and wore Cherokee cutoffs with towels wrapped around their shoulders. Even though I didn't know them, I still had to find a way to tap into my coolness. If I was lucky, I'd be written off as a freaky deaky dealer and left alone.

There was no time to waste. I put some primrose oil on to cover the stench of puke on my pink scarf. I didn't remember getting dressed and had no idea what I was wearing. I looked down into the mirror and saw my blue checked blouse and the gray wool skirt I wore to my father's viewing. I couldn't believe I was wearing a skirt. That was so unlike me. It made me look so girly and cute. To improve this doofus outfit, I rolled up the skirt to make it shorter and unbuttoned the shirt, then tied it up to let my belly show. That helped. Thank God, I had my bikini on underneath and my lucky rabbit foot was still attached.

I had to get home for Jean's morning check-in call. That was the drill when she worked nights. So no matter what, I was going to be home by nine fifteen. I had to hose off to make it seem like I'd just woken up and was on my way to the beach.

From the size of their big butts, I could tell these girls were from the Jonathan Club, a Republican, white-men only kind of place. If any girl got in there, it was just because her dad belonged. I had heard Rox and Claire dishing JC Girls when they thought I wasn't listening. They said they were pudgy, stuck-up little wannabes who brought way too much stuff to the beach. Even in the dim light, I saw an oversized radio and a backgammon board sticking out of their fishnet bags. No one in their right mind brought board games to the beach. That was total Kahala Hilton poolside behavior, but I guessed these rich bitches were trying to play down their privileged lives by using the public bathroom. They were amused by the gritty décor and the graffiti'd walls, but stopped dead in their tracks when they looked into the second stall. One by one, they pinched their noses, winced, and groaned in disgust. They leaned away and turned their faces in my direction.

I was almost out the entrance when, one by one, out of the corner of my eye, I saw them disappear into the open stalls. They were commenting on the graffiti, cackling as they tried figure out who or what "t-surfers" were. They had nasal, whiny voices and sounded so pathetic that for a moment I almost felt sorry for them. Some seagulls were screeching, fighting over a bag of chips the JCs had dropped. That was *really* lame. Trashing a beach wasn't cool.

I slipped my shades down and tried to walk casually without swaying. I could hear the girls' voices echoing from inside the bathroom as I turned toward the parking lot.

"Who the hell are the t-surfers?"

Obviously the JCs didn't know the rule about no foul language, but then again, it seemed on the mainland, girls could swear as long as long as no guys were around. I realigned my hair in the wind, took a deep breath, and started to haul.

If I was lucky, I'd get across PCH before the Dawn Patrol even got out of the water. No one would even know I had been to State.

CHAPTER FIFTEEN

t-surfers
In Retrograde

I'm not much into the solar system thing or stargazing. I don't bother breaking down the zodiac into planets and houses or strengths and weaknesses. Like I said, I just read *Sun Signs* and the astrology column in the newspaper. That gave me the information I needed. So I knew that yesterday Mercury went into retrograde. It does that for three weeks a few times a year and that's when everything goes spazzy.

Looking at the ground, there was no way to miss the two shadows looming a few feet in front of me. Out of nowhere, Rox and Claire were coming down the stairs. I backed up and tried to distance myself without running. I could hear their leather flip-flops clicking closer. I bent into the sand like a soldier dodging sniper bullets and made my way back to the bathroom. I stood flattening myself against the wall, palms opened wide, and waited.

The girls' bathroom was at the furthest end of the parking lot under two thin palm trees. There used to be three, but one burned down. To give the place privacy, a mauve peek-a-boo cinder block wall curved around it, blocking it from the rest of the beach. Some back stairs connected it to the parking lot area, but everyone entered from the State side.

Since when did Rox and Claire start sneaking onto the beach? It wasn't even 7:00 a.m. Was there some kind of girl convention going on I didn't know about? I checked around the corner. Rox and Claire were digging a hole under the stairs, scooping out wet sand and tossing black markers into it.

"No one will look here," Rox said.

They clicked their Styrofoam cups of coffee together and at the same time said, "Cheers."

So they were the t-surfer artists?

Even still, getting busted for trolling State so early wasn't an option. Neither was getting caught by Rox and Claire for spying on them. Both held fates worse than death.

Rox and Claire headed toward the bathrooms. I was jinxed. They were coming directly toward me. My head felt like it weighed a hundred pounds, and the back of my throat was raw. *Please Jesus, help me*, I pleaded in my head. I was trapped between the local goddesses and the JC big butts. There was no escape. I took a deep breath, pretended to be greasing up even though the sun had barely broken through the morning fog, fluffed my hair, and readied myself to BS them.

Claire cocked her head in my direction. She wore a hematite pink tube top and drawstring silk striped pajama pants that made her look like a butterfly when she moved. But

Rox was the full-on eye catcher. She wore a yellow muslin see-through shirt that blew tight against her body, showing off her golden skin and serving as the perfect backdrop for the double strands of plastic jade beads hanging over her breasts. Rox loved necklaces and wore them to the beach on important days. The Lisas had told me to pay close attention to what color Rox was wearing. It gave away her mood and tipped off the lineup as to what kind of day it would be. If she was wearing a necklace, look out. That meant something monumental was going to happen. From the looks of Rox that morning, something really important was going down, and I was right in the middle of it.

Rox stopped dead in her tracks and almost fell out of her bikini when she saw me. She put her hands on her hips and waited. I raised my finger to my mouth and smiled, shifting my eyes toward the bathroom. Rox understood my signal but crossed her arms tightly across her chest, pushing her boobs almost under her chin into her pissed-off pose again. No one told Rox to be quiet. I stood on one leg with the other knee bent, leaning my back against the wall as the JC Girls started ranting again about who the "†-surfers" were. They were breaking a rule that everyone but them seemed to know:

Never talk in the stalls.

Rox stiffened and walked toward me. Claire moved closer, too, poked me in the arm, and silently shrugged. I cupped my hand around her ear and whispered, "Jonathan Club."

"Who?" Rox asked.

"The Jonathan Club Turkeys," Claire answered. She continued, looking at me. "You know the only good thing about the Jonathan Club is that it's restricted."

That meant no black people or Jews. For the first time in my life, I worried about being too tan. Just when I thought I was beginning to understand how ruthless Claire was, she lowered the bar even further like in the limbo game, making it almost impossible to shimmy under it with her.

Rox was busy admiring her reflection in my shades as she mouthed the letters "JC" with a questioning look. I nodded. Then we smelled the pot wafting out of the bathroom vents and heard the JC Girls talking loudly about the ṭ-surfers. Rox put her hand on Claire's shoulder. Both of their mouths opened as they looked at each other and started to howl with laughter. Rox began acting like a spaz, mimicking the intruders in the bathroom who were still talking. She shouted, not caring how loud she was, "ṭ-surfers? ṭ-surfers?"

Claire jumped up and down as she watched Rox goof on the girls, laughing so hard she spit like a human geyser into the air. Then Rox grabbed Claire with such a force they fell butt-first into the sand, tears streaming down their faces. The smell of Noxzema and Ban Roll-On steamed off them as they collapsed into each other's arms singing together, "ṭ-surfers."

I wondered what was so funny about the "ṭ-surfers." I stayed cool, but when the JC Girls stormed out of the bathroom, I stepped back a bit.

One of them, wearing an ankle bracelet made of tiny Nepalese bells, hit a wet spot on the cement and slipped. Another girl reached out and tried to save her, but then they both went down hard. The two girls behind them tripped over them. The girl with the anklet had an elbow skinned to the bone and her friend's knees were bleeding. Rox and Claire were oblivious, rolling harder in the sand gasping for air.

The four girls untangled slowly. Sometimes, little gestures say more than words. When one of them flipped her hair quickly to the side, I knew something terrible was about to happen.

When Claire finally looked up, she had a strange expression on her face and Rox's eyes widened. The JC Girls towered over them. Rox sighed and Claire's grin faded from her face.

The JC Girls circled tighter around Rox and Claire. They seemed to think that Claire and Rox were nothing but silly pin-up girls who could be folded up and made to disappear. The one with the bloody knee lunged forward right into Claire's face and thumbed up her nose so it looked like a pig's snout. But the girl with bells around her ankle, the one I thought of now as Tinkerbell, yanked her back and stepped in front of her.

"They're mine," she said.

Tinkerbell was so muscular, she made Rox look awkward and gangly. She had on a Rolling Stones t-shirt without a bra, huge silver loop earrings, moccasin boots, shorts so tight she had a case of camel toe, and she had frizzy, dirty brown hair.

No one moved as Tinkerbell walked around Claire, psyching her out. I stayed totally still, trying not to draw attention to myself. There was something really wrong with this picture. I heard the JC Girls were usually digging for sand crabs or chasing sand pipers. I thought they wore Day-Glo green bikinis and sun block, drank chocolate milk, and ate shrimp cocktails.

"What's so funny about t-surfers?" Tinkerbell asked, raising her chin.

I was terrified that Rox and Claire would start laughing but they didn't. They stood up, dusted the sand off, and gave the JCs the silent treatment. It was their way of saying "up yours."

Rox and Claire used silence like a weapon, except this time it went on too long. It became like a dangerous fuse burning. I watched the four girls circle tighter around Claire and Rox, backing them out of sight from the rest of the beach.

In the daylight, they looked different. Tinkerbell was not a Jonathan Club debutante from the Coronet Ball, and her friends did not have swimming pool tans. They wore revealing tops with Fritz the Cat and the old pothead cartoon Mr. Natural on them. Their bikini bottoms tied to the side, making a bulge that looked like a muffin top over their shorts. Gross me out.

"What makes you think low-life Valley Dudes like you get to know anything?" Claire asked.

Dude was a country western word for people in checked shirts buttoned up to their necks, greased-back hair, cowboy boots, and cross-eye stares. It was banned on the beach and only used to describe a tourist, wannabe, or geek. No one, absolutely no one, wanted to be called a dude.

It all clicked. These weren't Jonathan Club Girls. They were the full-on rivals Mary Jo had warned me about, the ones who threw Molotov cocktails, those little sticks of dynamite, just to introduce themselves. Outside the bathroom, I could see the stuff in their fishnet bags more clearly. There was a Ouija board, not a backgammon one, and power blaster eight-track, not a radio. I was so totally screwed. These were total kick-your-ass *titas,* tough girls. That's what we called them back home. And judging from this bad call and the fact that Mercury was in retrograde, it looked like I'd probably never sit with the lineup again.

"What'd you steal?" Rox asked, pointing to Tinkerbell's purse.

Tinkerbell slapped the Styrofoam cup of coffee out of Rox's hand, but Rox didn't flinch.

"The Valley's that way," she snapped, pointing toward the freeway.

Tinkerbell looked like she was going to tear Rox apart, slice her to shreds, and then chew her up until only liquid oozed from her mouth. Claire tried to push Tinkerbell away, but the others held her back. I thought about something I learned from listening to soldiers at the Jones. In combat, hesitating is a deadly mistake. I was perched and ready to jump in. My fingers gripped tight into a fist as I watched the checkerboard in front of me shift again. I launched forward, staggering toward Rox, who motioned me back into a subordinate pose.

"We don't fight," she commanded.

"And we don't crash parties or try to screw other people's boyfriends, either," Claire said, standing right in Tinkerbell's face.

I felt a whole new kind of devotion to Rox and Claire as I leaned back against the wall and put my hands behind me. I was blown away by how they handled themselves.

"Your boyfriend's a freak," Tinkerbell snarled at Claire.

"Yeah, she totally got him off last night," Tinkerbell's friend chimed in. She was the one wearing a black t-shirt with cut off sleeves and the letters U.F.W.O.A. on the front. I had no idea what that meant but considering what a jerk she was, I figured it must have stood for Unfriendly Woman of America.

"You . . ." Claire almost called her a bitch, but Tinkerbell's sidekick pushed her in the sand, belly up. They were yelling and cheering over her.

That's when I started to talk to Jesus again. I didn't bother with Latin words or stained-glass images. I just cut to the chase and prayed, *Please help us. If you do, I won't watch TV for a month. Not even a commercial. I'll only watch the news with Jean. Please get us out of this.*

CHAPTER SIXTEEN

Banzai t-surfers

Maybe the vodka was giving me double vision, or maybe I was losing my mind. I peeked around the wall and looked toward the water. I saw two forms coming our way. I couldn't make out who they were, so I moved my head slowly back and forth the way I used to focus the lens of Dad's camera. I squinted with one eye and put a hand over the other. I moved away from Tinkerbell and Rox, who were standing toe to toe.

Through the mist hanging offshore, visions floated up the beach with wizard-like long hair flying behind them. They were two tall, Icelandic-looking gods with stomach muscles stacked on top of each other, totally buff. Both guys were more beautiful than any girl I had ever seen. Their faces had delicate features, strong jaws, and full lips. Another beauty with a dark tan joined them as they picked up their pace.

These were bona fide surf gods. They marched toward us with their boards tucked tight under their arms like knights heading into battle. As they got closer, it dawned on me that

I was looking at the McBride Twins, Nigel and Shawn, and the dark fish himself, Jerry Richmond.

There are only three things that can mess with a surfer's cool temperament: hunger, someone messing with his van, and seeing his chick in trouble. Judging from the look on Jerry's face, someone in the water must have told him the Vals were picking on Rox and Claire.

Jerry Richmond was notoriously mellow with a smile that made any girl feel like she was hearing the Carpenters sing. He looked like a rock star with his long dark mane and his perfect body without a single hair on it. On top of that, his biceps were the size of grapefruits and his Sundek trunks were tied so low, his groin muscles showed. As he walked closer through the morning breeze, he waved his arm at the twins, motioning for them to hurry up as they glided along over the sand. The slower they moved, the longer I'd get to stare at them. Unseen by the girls behind the wall, they made their way up the beach toward our spot by the bathroom. I remembered this rule:

Never make eye contact before he does.

Ordinarily, I would have had to rely on my peripheral vision or hide myself behind a veil of hair to get a good look at the McBrides and Jerry Richmond. But this was a crisis situation and because of that, an exception to the rule. The way things were right now, I figured I could look them straight on and not be considered a slut.

I'd never seen identical twins before, and the McBrides were hypnotic. There was no way to tell them apart, but

I knew that Shawn was Claire's. He wrote her love letters all the time, and he was sensitive. Nigel was a different story. He had a reputation for maneuvering girls smooth and easy, just the way he surfed. The only chink in the McBride's armor was that their number one devotion, even before surfing, was Jesus Christ. They were Born Again Christians who were saved right on State Beach, January 2, 1972, at a famous mass baptism. From what the Lisas told me, ever since then, the McBrides could out-surf anyone, except Jerry Richmond. The Lisas also told me that many girls had found the church thanks to Nigel. I couldn't imagine this. Just the same, Nigel and Shawn were hot.

Tinkerbell and her gang started whirling Rox and Claire around, making loud clucking noises.

No surfer went out with a girl who fought. Rox was twisting her elbow up to ward off Tinkerbell, who was flicking her finger at her face, trying to get her to fight back. None of them saw Jerry coming around the corner. He walked past me quickly and stuck the tip of his board right up the unexpecting Tinkerbell's butt. She jumped and started to kick, turning around quickly with her fist flying through the air, only to find Jerry, Nigel, and Shawn standing behind her. Tinkerbell immediately went into total sweet mode. It was bizarre. She dropped her shoulders, replaced her angry face with a cute smile, sucked in her stomach, and acted all coy, saying, "Good to see you again, Shawn."

"No, I'm Nigel," he answered, then pointed at his twin, "He's Shawn."

Jerry slipped his hand into Rox's and Shawn stood by Claire. The whole scene was weird. One minute, there was war going on and the next it was *Love, American Style*. Rox softened her scowl and smiled as Claire morphed into Little Miss Groovy. Just like that, the other girls uncrossed their arms as though they were all friends. From what Mary Jo had told me about these *titas* from the valley who like to beat up girls, an about-face like this was unheard of. What kind of gangsters were they?

Claire dug her toes into the sand as she backed up onto the open beach with Shawn. He wrapped his arm around her. His arm looked smooth, tan, and caked with salt from the ocean. It didn't matter that he was wet or that her tube top was getting soaked, cuddling was part of her girl duty. You *always* warmed your boyfriend, no matter what.

When Nigel entered the circle of Vals, a pulse pounded between my legs. There was no way to explain the feeling other than it reminded me of those nights when I locked the bathroom door. Nigel made me sober up instantly. I watched him make eye contact with every girl, luring them in one-by-one, then looking away and tossing each out like a scrap of bait. He looked fearless and unshakeable as he flipped his long hair and strolled over to Tinkerbell. Gently, he leaned his board against the bathroom wall as if it were made out of glass. He pulled his red trunks down so none of us saw anything dangling under the waistband.

What a hunk. I pinched the back of my neck to stop myself from grinning. If I laughed, giggled, or even smiled it would have been worse than my goof-up of not recognizing the Vals in the bathroom. I dug my fingernails into my arm and prayed again. *Please, Jesus. Help me keep my shit together.*

"You're a wild man," Tinkerbell said to Nigel.

"Yeah," her buddy said.

Tinkerbell positioned herself in front of Nigel with her back to Rox and Claire. She grabbed his arm and pulled him to her.

"What's the problem?" he asked.

He leaned in closer to the group of girls. From the grin on his face, I could tell he was enjoying the way they were coming on to him.

"We just want to know something," Tinkerbell's friend said while she put her arm around Nigel. Her jean shorts were so tight, she had a camel toe, too.

"We want to know why the t-surfers rule," Tinkerbell cooed.

Claire watched carefully as Rox sashayed around them like a cat about to kill. I could almost see her tail twitching.

"Ask Nani," she said, pointing in my direction. "She'll tell you who the t-surfers are."

I felt my voice slide down my throat and land somewhere in my gut. I had no clue who the t-surfers were. My heart snapped apart and felt like it was hanging by a single thin vein. I thought I was having a heart attack. They all looked at me. A nasty taste rose from my stomach. It was those gherkins again.

The weird thing is it was Tinkerbell who rescued me. She motioned for her *titas* to make their move into the bathroom. All of them were flirting and teasing the guys. The

Vals were total scum buckets and all they really wanted to do was piss off Rox and Claire. They were all good prick teasers, but Tinkerbell was the best. She moved in on Jerry again, touched the tip of his board, leaned on him, and lit his smoke. Even more amazing, she tried to push Rox out of the way and gave Jerry a little tug toward the bathroom.

"Just look inside," she said in her best come-get-me voice.

But Jerry wouldn't leave Rox's side. Shawn looked worried, like he'd catch a venereal disease or something if he went into the girl's bathroom. He shook his head, no.

"I'll go with you," Tinkerbell's friend said to him.

Shawn would not budge. The fight was officially over, but the fun was just beginning. Nigel wasn't freaked out. He let the Valleys pull him into the bathroom. He poked his head around the corner.

Nigel McBride was even better looking from the rear. His ass was tiny, and as he turned his body side to side, every muscle in his back rippled. Nigel was also a ham, a total goofball. He held out his thumb, like a painter trying to get perspective. Rox and Claire giggled, but when I laughed, they growled at me. What did I do wrong? That is, besides confuse the meanest bunch of girls in the world with the dumbest ones and not tell Rox and Claire that their boyfriends were coming up the beach? Aside from that, I should be in the clear.

"We're waiting," Tinkerbell squawked.

No one else noticed the dirty looks I was getting. They were too busy watching Nigel do his Michelangelo imitation. He was tilting his head side to side, admiring the graffiti but not going all the way into the bathroom. Nigel turned with a big smile on his face.

"Hey, you guys should check this out."

"No way, José," Jerry said.

Both Shawn and Jerry hugged their babes and gave him a thumbs down.

"Well, I can tell you who the ƚ-surfers are," he announced, turning to me. "If Nani doesn't mind."

Nigel McBride said my name. He *knew* my name. And he was still smiling.

"Absolutely," I said. Don't ask me how I got a four-syllable word out without slurring.

It might seem like nothing, but it was a turning point in my life. When Nigel McBride talked to me, the world changed. Maybe that Jesus stuff was working. I felt protected, like a lucky charm had floated into my lap. Then bang. The sound of Tinkerbell snapping a huge bubble brought me back to earth.

"Come on, we're waiting," she commanded.

No one bossed around the most prominent surfer at State. Especially someone from the valley with hair that looked like it got stuck in an electrical socket. Tinkerbell brazenly lit a cigarette and tossed the match into the sand. Nigel said, "Mistake."

She acted like she didn't hear him and took such a long drag that it totally hot-boxed her Marlboro. What was wrong with this fool? Anyone with half a brain knew girls weren't supposed to sass.

**Girls listen, look pretty, and compliment guys.
Especially surfers.**

That rule dominated all others. But Tinkerbell and her stoners didn't care. They thought they were moving in again but must have forgotten that State Beach was sort of like Nicaragua. I mean, it wasn't a good place to visit.

"Jesus Christ, Nigel . . ." Tinkerbell said.

Nigel zoned her. The small talk was over. Without giving Tinkerbell a chance to continue, he said, "It's Christian Surfers, not t-surfers. Christian Surfers Rule. It's a cross, not a 't,' you nimrod."

Shawn began to chant, holding one finger high in the sky, "Christian surfers rule. Christian surfers rule."

Jerry joined in. Nigel held up the crucifix hanging around his neck so close to Tinkerbell's face that her hobbit-like eyes crossed. She jumped back, trying to focus, and bumped his board. It fell to the ground. The crowd went silent.

Everybody froze, watching Nigel's board bounce on the cement. Shawn ran to its side like it was a child who had just been hit by a car, inspected every inch, and announced, "No dings."

Rox and Claire had huge grins on their faces when Nigel walked toward Tinkerbell, moving her out farther and farther onto the open beach. He yelled, "Go back to the valley, you bimbo!"

Jerry joined in by snapping his wet towel at her.

"Let's go," said Tinkerbell's friend.

She reached for Tinkerbell, who winced when her elbow was touched. It was a bloody mess.

Tinkerbell would never be allowed on State again. She had blown it for life. Getting shined on by the McBrides and Jerry Richmond was not something any girl, no matter how tough she was, could come back from. Her friends hurried her off the beach, reeling from a moment she would never ever live down. When she passed me, everyone saw her deliberately bump me hard against the wall. I almost started to cry.

Tinkerbell scampered off the beach. Nigel walked toward me. I fiddled with the tips of my hair and looked the other way so that I could mellow out. When I turned back, I caught Tinkerbell's eye. She stuck her chin in the air and slowly drew her finger across her neck like a hunting knife. Why was she threatening me instead of Rox and Claire? Nigel stopped right in front of me. To keep my legs from quivering, I pressed my knees together and waited. I wanted to say something, but I remembered the rule:

Don't talk to a guy until he talks to you.

I could smell the ocean and Mr. Zog's Sex Wax on his body. He stood close enough for me to reach out and touch one of his hard little nipples. I didn't move an inch. I couldn't breathe. Nigel dashed forward and scooped a bottle cap up from the sand. With a smirk on his face, Nigel gave me a wink, then leaned forward and took aim. He flicked the cap so it hit Tinkerbell right between her shoulders. That thing had so much zip on it, you could hear it whizzing by in the air. Probably thinking a bee stung her, she screeched and flailed her arms around like a windmill. Her *titas* came to her rescue and started shooing the phantom away. I had to look toward the sand to keep myself from losing it.

Nigel was totally mind-boggling. His hair was halfway down his back, and there was a tiny dimple in his chin. I felt a surge of heat erupt. He lifted up my Don Ho wraparound shades and gently placed them on top of my head. The sun hit me like a strobe light, splitting my brain apart. I was dizzy but couldn't keep from smiling as I looked into his dark blue eyes. My mind went blank: a white slate of nothingness. I didn't think about my dad or Jean, Rox or Claire, Hawaii or the mainland, 33 Sage or the Java Jones. At that very moment, there was nothing in the world but Nigel McBride.

"Cool eyes," he said softly.

Oh my God, he liked my hazel-green eyes. I went on total autopilot and did everything Annie taught me, including wetting my lips with my tongue before biting down on the bottom one ever so slightly.

"We're going to Roy's," Jerry yelled to Nigel.

Nigel just kept looking at me. He tugged at my skirt and said, "Do you go to Marymount? Is this your uniform? You smell like vanilla."

I nodded yes even though all the answers were no, and I was wearing primrose oil.

"Nigel, are you coming?" Shawn asked with a hint of frustration in his voice.

"I think he is," Jerry laughed as he watched Nigel lean into me and sniff again. It wasn't gross like when Lord Ricky smelled me. When Nigel sniffed, it tickled and made the short hairs on my arms rise.

Rox gave Jerry a little bump with her hip. They looked so hot together. I could tell how much she loved him because her face softened and her eyebrows relaxed when he was near her.

Rox took Claire by the hand and together they walked around Jerry's board, strolling my way. Nigel had redeemed my status when he shifted his interest toward me. Rox spun around and leaned on the wall while Claire stood on my other side.

"We'll all meet you at Roy's," Rox said.

"Wanna go?" Nigel asked me.

Me? Go to Roy's? Was Nigel McBride asking me to go to Roy's like I was one of them or something?

When I looked at Nigel, I thanked Jesus. It had to be Jesus making all of this happen or maybe Mercury wasn't in retrograde yet. Or maybe it was just my lucky day.

CHAPTER SEVENTEEN

Sucked Over the Lip

On the corner of Pacific Coast Highway and Entrada Drive LOCALS ONLY was spray painted across the sidewalk. That was the front of Roy's, a tiny brick shack that used to be a train station before roads were put in. If you didn't know Roy's was there, you'd never find it. Except for the dogs. There must have been at least fifteen shepherd mixes lounging on the front steps, baking in the sun, waiting for their masters.

No one, absolutely no one, got a seat inside without knowing someone. For a girl, walking into Roy's for the first time was the ultimate introduction into surf society. The equivalent of what the Jonathan Club debutants called "being presented."

The sun-flooded restaurant was packed after the morning session. It reeked of cigarette smoke, bacon, and coffee. My stomach was still in a knot, but the food smelled good. How could I be hungry? While struggling to figure out my next move, I remembered the rule:

Never eat in front of guys.

"Good morning, ladies," Roy said from behind the counter. He looked like a big, fat Elvis in an apron. "They're in the back," he continued.

Shawn waved Rox and Claire over to the booth. I followed. Claire took Rox's hand and started winding her way through the deafening noise of hoots, hollers, and whistles. There must have been fifty guys jammed in that tiny restaurant. All of them were various hues of blonde. Unreal.

I imagined the tide pulling me out. I let smiles wash over me like the sea. In this surf grotto, guys still had pillowcase creases on their cheeks and uncombed, wet hair. They were all murky and moist, wrapped up in towels and sweatshirts. Some surfers looked cool in plaid jackets two sizes too small, unzipped low-slung cords, Birdie trunks, and visors facing backward. It didn't matter what they wore. They were all wizards to me.

Inside the sanctuary, Rox and Claire gazed down at their admirers like the high priestess and empress they were and eased their way to the back of the restaurant. Corky Carroll and his Orange County–Costa Mesa guys gave Claire "the nod." He raised his cup of coffee and asked Rox, "Is Rincon going off?"

Was Rincon before San Diego or after Ventura? I couldn't remember. I had to learn these things. But it was more important at that moment not to frown, fret, or look like a spaz, so I put both my hands behind my back, just above my hips, and held onto the tips of my hair for dear life.

Rox stopped and thought about the question. She looked at Claire and they whispered to each other. She eventually gave Corky a wink and said, "Yes."

The place went bananas. How could I learn to wink like that? I looked at Claire for a clue about what to do next but it was too late. The game was on. She was too busy being Claire. Lord Ricky stood up and announced, "Finish up, lads. We're heading north." He pushed his way forward and said, "Corky, this is Nani, David Nuuhiwa's cousin."

Corky Carroll took my hand and kissed it.

"No hard feelings?" he asked looking into my eyes.

Assuming he was referring to a rumor that he had snaked "my cousin" David out of a surf championship in Huntington Beach a few years back, I shook my head and said, "It's cool."

Never take on a guy's fight.

That rule was a good one. A no-brainer, really. It was dangerous to get in the middle of a surf war, especially between a rock star mainlander and an island bad boy. All I wanted was to make it to the booth where Nigel, Shawn, and Jerry were holding court. A waitress in a pink uniform with DARLENE written on her nametag placed three orders of toast, four plates of pancakes, and two cheese omelets on the table. She had a red beehive hairdo, a round body, and wore too much black eye liner. She was the perfect match to go with Roy.

After pouring coffee for three other tables, she gave me a little shove with her big hips.

"If you stand still," she said, "they'll eat you alive."

Rox and Claire had waltzed through the crowd and landed next to Jerry and Shawn while I was stuck like a deer caught in headlights. Guys were looking at my ass like it was a Hawaiian delicacy of soaked sweet meat.

Weaving my way through a maze of syrup-drenched fingers trying to touch me, I got a sinking feeling in my gut. It was kind of like the way a surfer must feel before getting sucked over the lip. Inside Roy's, just like inside a wave, things could go wrong fast.

There wasn't room in the booth. I stood there like an idiot wondering where to go. Nigel sat with his back to me in a chair at the head of the table. He ate whole pancakes one at a time and didn't seem to know I was there. I felt invisible. I said, "I better get going."

I was like a surfer who got pulled under a monster wave lost at sea and not knowing which way was up and which way was down. I prayed for enough air to navigate the crowded aisles and make it to the sunlight beyond the door. When I turned to leave, I noticed Rox tap Jerry, Jerry jab Shawn, and Shawn elbow Nigel. Just then, a long arm reached out and pulled me back. Nigel had me on his lap before my feet had ever moved. He grabbed me around the waist, spread his legs, pulled me down, and, without missing a beat, placed half a strip of bacon in my mouth. With his wet trunks nestled around my thighs, my mind raced. What now? I had to think Virgo. First times are my specialty. After all, Virgo means virgin. All I needed to do was stay level and be sweet.

Nigel rested his arm on the outside of my thigh for the whole restaurant to see. I had just become a full-on citizen of State Beach. No one, not a gargoyle, stupid mother, or

BS-ing uncle could stop me now. Like getting a permanent visa, it was a done deal.

Nigel passed me the last sip of his orange juice, and I drank from the glass as if it was the Holy Grail. The juice burned my raw throat and made me want to gag, but I smiled anyway. I don't think I'll ever be able to enjoy orange juice again. Nigel hadn't actually talked to me yet, but when he reached for the salt, he buried his nose deep into my neck and inhaled just below my earlobe. He pulled me in close and wrapped my hair around his shoulders like a cape. Rox and Claire smiled approvingly as Jerry blurted out to those seated around the table, "Ready?"

Everyone wiggled out of the tiny booth. I could see Shawn's reflection in the window as he nudged his brother and made some cryptic comments in the secret language of twins. Nigel turned and smiled at me.

"Wanna come?" he asked.

Before I could answer, he took my hand and led me out of Roy's.

Entrada Drive was backed up with beach traffic going to State. Suzie's convertible bug was the last in line at the red light. Jenni rode copilot, and Mary Jo sat in the back. The three of them turned around so fast it looked like they got whiplash when they saw Nigel put his arm around me. We walked right next to her car. At first Suzie smiled. Then it must have dawned on her: Nigel McBride and I were together. She looked away. Both her hands gripped the wheel and Jenni patted her bare shoulder, consoling her. Mary Jo, always the Leo, called out, "Welcome back, Nigel. Where ya heading?"

Nigel was giving a guy directions and barely responded to her question except for flashing her a quick smile.

Mary Jo was delighted, but Suzie kept her eyes forward, waiting for the light to change. It was really weird. It looked like she was going to cry or something. At the Chevron Station, a bunch of boys were jumping over curbs and doing handstands on their skateboards. Nigel and I enjoyed the show. These kids were totally radical, mondo cool, like nothing I'd ever seen in Hawaii. In fact, no one skateboarded or hula hooped anymore back home. These boys were outrageous. Each board was like sawed off wood perfectly shaped on clay wheels. Their cutback moves and hand turns were fearless as they plowed through broken glass in bare feet.

"Go back to Revere," Jerry scolded one of the boys. The kid flipped him off and kept skating.

"Paul Revere is the local junior high school," Nigel told me.

Jerry returned the finger and smiled. The boys and him seemed to have an understanding.

"Aren't they cute?" Jerry asked me.

Shawn and Nigel were putting their boards into a baby blue VW van parked in the NO PARKING zone with several other vans at the gas station.

"This is the VIP spot," Shawn told me. He hopped into the back of the van. It looked dark and mysterious. There was a thin mattress with more boards stacked around it. Wet suits hung on wire hangers and towels were tossed everywhere. Nigel was clearing off the front seat, tossing empty beer bottles into a rusted trash can. Rox talked to Claire in her hush-hush voice as the bottles hit the bottom of the can and clanked loudly.

"What are we going to tell Suzie?" Claire asked.

Rox looked slightly annoyed with the question. She said, "Nigel made the choice, we're neutral." She waved at Suzie, who was finally turning onto PCH, letting the tears fall as she downshifted.

Shawn handed Claire his board while he arranged the others in the back of the van. Holding his surfboard was an honor only she got. Rox on the other hand, stood with her shirt blowing open, making cars screech to a stop on the highway, enjoying every near wreck.

"Why's Suzie crying?" I asked.

Claire looked me straight in the eyes.

She said, "Suzie did it with Nigel before he went to Ensenada. She was kind of hoping they'd get together when he got back. But," she beamed, "looks like he changed his mind."

Duh, I thought to myself, *Nigel was Suzie's secret guy.* Shawn sailed past us into the back of the van. He made himself comfortable on half of the bed. Claire followed. Jerry and Rox took the other half of the foam mattress. There was a rule, a very, very important rule, that I had just accidentally broken.

Never snag another girl's boyfriend.

Rox leaned forward before she slammed the back door shut.

She said, "Don't worry about it. He wasn't hers. They weren't totally together. Just get in the van."

Like she could read my mind or something.

Nigel was holding the passenger door open for me.

"Let's go," he said. He held my hand as I stepped up into the front seat like I was stepping onto a throne.

I was blown away but still worrying. It was eight forty-five. I had to be home at nine fifteen to check-in with Jean.

"Hey, McBride," Lord Ricky sang out. "Going to Rincon? Got rooma for meya?"

Lord Ricky leaned in through the passenger window. We both sort of jumped back when we saw each other. It was the first time I got to see him up close when he wasn't yelling. If it weren't for those accidents that left him with a scar across his lip and a gash down his cheek, he'd definitely have a really nice face. I could tell he was probably cute once upon a time, maybe about three windshields ago. Nigel signaled for him to get in the back of the van.

Rox and Claire giggled as he squeezed between them and rocked the van up and down. Nigel cranked up the radio, putting all the sound into the back. Lord Ricky reached behind my ear and pulled out the "get out of jail free" card from Monopoly.

"Magic," he said.

I love magic and tricks.

"You might need this," Lord Ricky said and flicked the card into Nigel's lap. Nigel flinched and stuck the card into the glove compartment. He grabbed my knee and held it tight before shifting the van into reverse.

Lord Ricky dipped below the curtains that divided the front seat from the back. When he totally disappeared, he made an exaggerated sneeze, "Jailbait."

Nigel looked in the rearview mirror. "Shut up, Rick," he said.

For one second, I was happy. Then I wasn't. Did he know I was only fifteen? And I remembered Rincon was by Santa Barbara, almost two hours north of State. How the hell was I going to get home in time?

I turned up the radio. Van Morrison was singing "Tupelo Honey." I prayed that no one in the back would hear me.

"Hey, Nigel," I said, "Uh, I can't go."

Now I had to come up with a reason that he would understand and still want to see me again. It had to be something that would get his sympathy but not freak him out. It also had to be a one-time only excuse.

"Why?" he asked, yanking the parking brake up.

"It's my dad's obituary. I have to read it to my mom."

Nigel looked away.

"She didn't see it before she left for St. John's," I said, struggling to sound believable.

"Is she sick, too?" he asked.

"No, she's fine. She works there. It's just she couldn't bring herself to see it before we left Hawaii, and I promised her I'd read it to her when she was ready."

"I didn't know," he said and leaned his forehead on the steering wheel. Little pink patches appeared on Nigel's skin. He looked like he was upset.

All of a sudden everything changed. I was comforting him. Nigel felt soft as he put his head on my shoulder and said, "I'm so sorry about your dad, Nani."

Nigel McBride was only the second person that had ever said those comforting words to me and actually meant it. Back home, people said them to Jean all the time, but nobody ever said them to me except Annie. I was the poor *hapa haole* who only got sad looks. Well, I wished they could see me now. Here I was in the arms of Nigel McBride, the coolest guy in California.

We sat in silence and Nigel kept holding me. We were so close, it felt like we had melted into one. It had been so long since I'd felt the comfort of strong arms. It made me think of my dad.

"Hi," Jerry said, looking like a puppet as he stuck just his head out from under the curtains. His lips were so close to mine I could smell traces of Rox's Sen-Sens breath fresheners on them. I could also see something about him that I hadn't noticed before. His eyes were slanted up slightly. He looked more mixed than I did and he had stubble on his chin.

"Are we going soon?" he asked matter-of-factly.

Jerry's voice was smooth like a slide guitar. Annie Iopa had made surfers out to be impatient or Lord Ricky–types who just wanted to ride waves and get blown. But these guys were different. Could it be the Jesus factor? If it was, I really owed the "Stick God" one. That's what my dad used to call Jesus because he was almost always mounted on wood.

"After we take Nani home," Nigel told everybody else listening in the van.

It was unheard of for a surfer to make a detour when there were waves. Nigel didn't know where I lived, but it didn't seem to matter. He was taking me home even if it was out of the way.

"33 Sage, down just a few blocks," I said.

Rox and Claire didn't question the change of plans, but Jerry was clearly stoked to hear I lived close by. Lord Ricky lit up a joint. I passed it to Nigel as he pushed in a Jethro Tull eight-track. Before "Aqualung" finished, I was home.

CHAPTER EIGHTEEN

Sucked [2]

For the first time in my life, I felt like a normal girl. Nigel McBride was a perfect slice of American cheese. The Lisas had told me all about his parents who were at the top of a group called the Fortune 500. That meant they were rich. I didn't really care about money, but I knew it was better to have it than not.

Mr. McBride was a big Nixon supporter. He and Mrs. McBride had five other grown children from their long, bad marriage. The Lisas told me Mrs. McBride always wore her Kappa Alpha Theta pin and her sparkly diamond necklace that was a Betty Ross Award she got for being the Outstanding Republican Woman of 1970. Rumor had it that, in the world of politics, she was even more powerful than Mr. McBride.

In one morning, I had found the cure for all my troubles. Nigel made me forget about *Playboy* Bunnies, *Barbarella*, Rox, and Claire and all the awful news Jean forced me to watch, like students getting killed at Kent State and Vietnamese kids drenched in napalm running naked. In the blink of an eye, I was no longer crying over the sale of the Java Jones or the death of my dad. Hawaii didn't even seem to matter so much anymore. Everything bad or sad went away, and just like that, I was okay. I wasn't a *Funny Kine* after all. I liked boys. I liked them full-on, totally and for sure. I was normal, and I'd never be alone.

Behaving ladylike, or *ho'owahine* as Dad called it, meant waiting. Nigel stood in the middle of a bunch of overgrown wisteria tugging at my door and finally opening it.

"I'll see you in," he said.

There were a few groans from the back of the van as the door slid open and smoke billowed out. Rox and Claire looked like they just woke up, eyes at half-mast and hair everywhere.

"Take care, Nani," Claire mumbled.

"Sorry about your folks, I mean, your dad," Rox joined in.

"Me, too," Shawn shrugged.

"Yeah," Jerry said, closing the door quietly so Lord Ricky wouldn't wake up.

They were stoned and had obviously heard every word of my excuse. But I knew it was all cool when Nigel followed me up the stairs. We walked to the back door and everything wrong with 33 Sage leapt out at me: the broken window screen, the old wicker chair with stuffing sticking out of its cushion, and the seriously overgrown bougainvillea. Nigel seemed oblivious to all of it. After untangling himself from Jean's bizarre security system of rusted cowbells in the orange trees, I told him that making noise when entering a home is a Hawaiian tradition for good luck. That was completely bogus, but I didn't know how else I could explain these obnoxious things and save face. Anyway, he seemed to buy it.

Nigel escorted me all the way into the house through the kitchen. He didn't notice the dirty dishes piled next to the sink or the slew of Mayfair Market bags splayed all over the counter or the smell of overripe bananas lying next to the Yuban Coffee can filled with bacon grease or the mismatched chairs around our table. Nigel didn't even hear my new fish tank buzzing or see that there were no fish inside or notice that the glass was already covered by algae.

I questioned Nigel's vision for real when he walked into the living room and nonchalantly passed the TV tray with Jean's smelly slippers on it, not to mention the ashtray overflowing with cigarette butts. He saw absolutely nothing through those beautiful eyes but a small black-and-white photograph resting on the shelf.

"Is this you?" he asked, holding the photo in his hand.

I nodded. It was Dad's favorite of me with Duke Kahanamoku. Nigel looked like he had just seen Jesus Christ himself. I was ready for him drop to his knees and start talking in tongues.

I hadn't peed since before sunrise. It was a world record, but I couldn't hold it another second without getting permanent brain damage. While Nigel ogled at the photo of Duke Kahanamoku, I casually announced that I had to let the cat out. Nigel didn't look up and I ran to the back of the house. We didn't have a cat but he'd never know that.

The water was still swishing down the toilet when I opened the bathroom door. Nigel was looking around my room. I hoped he hadn't heard me pee. It was a rule:

Never let a guy hear you pee or fart.

Nigel picked up Mrs. Beasley. He fussed with her yellow hair and fiddled with her glasses. He looked at me coyly and then lifted her polka-dot skirt but didn't see the white threaded seam across her belly that looked just like Jean's cesarean scar. He cha cha'd with Mrs. Beasley across the room, twirling her around, cuddling her close to his chest. I didn't think it could get more embarrassing until he noticed the string. I prayed he wouldn't pull it but he did. Mrs. Beasley said, "Do you wanna play?"

Mrs. Beasley sounded drunk and slow. Not squeaky and happy like she was supposed to.

Nigel laughed. Then he pulled the string again and these words came out of Mrs. Beasley. "If you could have three wishes, what would you wish for?"

My first wish would be that Nigel stop making Mrs. Beasley talk. My second wish would be that I'd get the nerve to sprinkle Dad's ashes at State. It was clear that the longer I waited, the more trouble I'd have. The third wish would be that Nigel McBride would fall madly in love with me.

Something else caught Nigel's eye. On the wall, right where Jean had put them, were the pictures of Jesus. Nigel stared at the Jesus with his palms held above his head and the sacred heart on his chest. He touched the plastic glow-in-the-dark rosary hanging over the frame and asked, "Have you accepted Jesus?" He looked stunned.

Jerry was honking the horn outside. Nigel ignored it. He flipped back his damp hair and tightened the towel around his waist. Absentmindedly, he stroked his chest while staring at me real hard. Was I in trouble? He looked so stern.

I guess I had accepted Jesus. I mean, I'd been talking to him all morning. I didn't see any harm in saying yes. But just in case, I crossed my fingers under my hair.

"*Iesu*, in Hawaiian," I added.

Nigel walked toward me and softly said, "That's so hot. Say it again."

"*Iesu.*"

"Again."

"*Iesu.*"

He slowly backed me up against the wall. I rested my head as he took the tips of my hair and bit down on them. I relied on the cool plaster instead of my legs to keep me steady. Nigel was really tall. I held my chin up and stood on my tiptoes just to keep in front of his eyes. He pressed into me and swayed side to side. I wasn't sure what to do.

I didn't know very much about this stuff. I only knew that it would probably be best for me to kiss him before navigating the rest of his body. I put my hand behind Nigel's neck and pulled his head toward my lips. As he got close, I tilted my head back slightly and opened my mouth. I reminded myself of what Annie told me: to keep my lips relaxed while gently pushing my tongue into his mouth. I was cool because I had practiced it a thousand times on marshmallows while watching reruns of *I Love Lucy*. But when Nigel slipped his tongue around mine, it felt a whole lot different than a marshmallow.

I had only officially kissed two guys, but this was nothing like playing spin the bottle with Eli Kalili, or when Stuart Wong had a crush on me and talked me into having a séance with him in his bathroom. Calling back Kui Lee from the dead was a good excuse to get in the dark, light a candle, and make out. That was in fifth grade when I was still fat.

Kissing Nigel was way different. I felt transported to another world where silk curtains moved in slow motion and soft music played. He wrapped one hand around my waist, pressed his bare chest into me, and lifted my skirt with his free hand just like he had on Mrs. Beasley. I was imagining floating toward clouds filling the morning sky when the phone rang. Then it rang again and again.

I looked at Nigel's watch. It was 9:15 a.m. on the dot. Time for Jean's check-in call. My hair was pinched between my back and the wall. Nigel had me sandwiched; I was stuck. The phone kept ringing as I grabbed my hair with both hands and pulled it to one side, freeing myself with just enough room to roll out of Nigel's arms. I ran down the hall fast as I could to the living room and grabbed the receiver.

"Hello."

Nigel dashed behind me and, as I listened to Jean go off about Uncle Mike, St. John's, and what we would have for dinner that night, Nigel handed me a copy of my dad's obituary. How he had seen that newspaper buried in all the junk in my room was a mystery. He stood close to me with a raised eyebrow and a hard-on. What the hell was I going to do? Actually, I had no choice. I rested the phone on my shoulder and Nigel took my hand.

"Mom, I am going to read Dad's obituary now," I said, unable to even imagine her response.

When none came, I continued, "James Kamalei Nuuhiwa, 'Jimmy Star' to his friends, died today, April 15, 1972, at his home in Kaimuki. He was forty-two. The owner of Waiki-ki's famous entertainment bar, the Java Jones, where artists Haunani Kahalewai, Hilo Hattie, Lani Kai, Alfred Apaka, Gilbert 'Zulu' Kauhi, Pakalolo, and the late, great, Kui Lee performed regularly. Jimmy had a wonderful sense of humor and a positive outlook on life. He was a native Hawaiian and is survived by many generations of the Nuuhiwa family. Jimmy was a great storyteller and his presence will be missed by all, especially at Sunday surfing and Wednesday volleyball with the Royal Hawaiian Regulars. Jimmy's call to God came from a fatal heart attack. He is survived by his wife Jean Nuuhiwa, a native Californian, and their daughter, Haunani Grace Nuuhiwa, as well as long-time business partner Michael Kei. There will be no paddle out. A private memorial will be held for family and friends."

I could hear Jean crying on the phone. I don't know what came over me.

While looking up at Nigel, I told Jean, "I love you."

The words just fell out of my mouth. Tears welled up in my eyes until they poured down my face and onto Nigel's chest. I had always been able to hold them back, but feeling Nigel's hands around my waist somehow got to me and the leak turned into a flood. There was a rule, of course:

Never lose it in front of a guy you like.

Jean cried hard while telling me, "Honey, sweetheart, I love you, too."

She hadn't said a nice word to me in months. It brought up those old feelings I had for her when she was the best mom in the world. This sent me over the edge.

Nigel looked freaked out. My tears streaked his salt-stained chest. He gave me a weird look and walked toward the door. Oh God, could he have thought I was saying, "I love you" to him? I mean, I did say it to him, but I meant it for Jean.

Jean wasn't used to me being so emotional. She told me she'd be home soon and we would talk. What was I thinking? I studied every move on Nigel's face to see how badly I had blown it. I knew it wasn't good when he backed farther away.

"Bye," I said to Jean. I hung up the phone.

"Bye," Nigel said to me.

I could tell from his eyes that he *did* think I said, "I love you" to him. They didn't have that sleepy cool look anymore, and the magnetic pull that made me feel like I was floating off the ground was gone. There was an awkward silence. Nigel fumbled with the front door lock a couple of times. He looked worried as I moved closer to help him. We stood toe to toe.

"I'm going to pray for your family," he said. And then, in an instant, he vanished through the shrubs.

CHAPTER NINETEEN

✳

Heart Attack

I was hiding in my tent in the drop-and-cover position. On my knees, hands locked behind my neck. I rocked back and forth with my chin tucked deep into my chest. In my head, I could still hear Dad slamming the screen door and shuffling over the gravel drive to his car.

My dad's heart attack happened so fast. By the look on his face, I thought he had a sour stomach or indigestion. I watched him leave the house from my bedroom window. He was drinking a bottle of Pepto-Bismol and lighting up a joint. He was rubbing his forehead like it hurt really badly and rested for a moment. I was just about to yell out, "Are you okay, Daddy?" when he fell like a tree cut in one swift chop.

He clutched his left arm, dropped to his knees, and rolled onto his side. When I got to him, he had curled into a little ball; he was breathing hard, and the skin under his eyes had turned blue. He didn't know who I was. A pasty film covered his face. I didn't know what to do. I touched his hands. They were cold and wet. He was totally confused and talking gibberish—that's when I screamed for my mom. The muscles on his face pulled tight and his eyes rolled back. He smelled like wet cement, quivering gray. I tried to yank him to one side but fell under his weight.

Jean ran out of the house yelling, "Call an ambulance!"

She pushed me aside so hard I fell on my hip.

Before the ambulance left our house, Daddy was in a coma. They call his kind of heart attack a "widow maker." When they hit, a person is lucky because they die fast. Yeah, *real lucky*.

It felt like I had a thousand heart attacks in the two days since Nigel left. I think I got plaque in my arteries or something like that from all the stress. I remember the ambulance guy made it really easy to understand. He told me the heart is like a city and the arteries are like roads. And now my roads were collapsing, just like my dad's. If I could stop thinking about how badly I blew it with Nigel, maybe the heart attacks would end.

Jean's face was in her bottomless tumbler of wine. She didn't notice I had gone underground, and she had totally forgotten any tender moments from the days before. She was too busy now having a meltdown about Angela Davis getting out of jail. I was a total nonissue.

I figured it would be best to duck out from State for a while. My dream chamber had turned into a hard shell, cold and murky. So I found a new place to hide, a real place. I made my primo tent by running a sheet from the pegboard of my hobby center to the end of my bed. There was just enough room inside for my sleeping bag and record player.

That was cool because I had been listening to Joni Mitchell's *Ladies of the Canyon* drone on since Thursday. I kept pushing the replay button with my big toe. I wanted to die to the sound of her voice.

It wasn't time for lunch or dinner, but Jean was cooking again. She got adventurous on her days off. The scent of ham steaks and pineapple frying on the hibachi wafted through my window and into my tent. Jean had taken to soaking everything she cooked in white wine, and she kept her tumbler with her at all times just in case she needed extra flavoring. At night, she'd wander around her weird little garden balancing her checkbook, doing the math on her fingers, and sitting by a kerosene lamp waiting for an occasional moth to go up in flames.

Jean was upset because Uncle Mike wasn't returning her calls. She stood at the kitchen sink watching for the mailman, waiting for a check, sales slip, or something from the Java Jones.

I think there was something wrong with the mail. I hadn't gotten a postcard or anything from Annie in over a week.

In addition to having heart attacks, I hadn't brushed my teeth since I kissed Nigel. If that wasn't lame enough, I hadn't had the strength to shave my legs or open a new bottle of Breck to wash my hair. The best I could do was put on a clean muumuu and ask Jean to barbecue me a Spam burger. Unfortunately, that reminded the nut job of my father, which got her crying again. It was probably best to just stay in the tent, put on another Joni Mitchell record, and dream.

Sometimes the pain in my chest went away. And I'd think of the look on Nigel's face when he left. Then the pain would come right back. If I could only figure out what sign he was, maybe I'd know what went wrong. He was sensitive and sweet like a Libra, but sexy and strong like a Scorpio. Or maybe he was a Capricorn. It was too much to think about. I started praying. I switched between Jesus and Pele. Finally, I did a quick round of eeny, meeny, miny, moe to decide which one would be my god for the day. Out went Pele.

I asked Jesus to give me another chance with Nigel. The breeze blew smoke from the grill into my room. I got up. I considered setting up the TV trays and eating with Jean, but I knew that would only make me sadder. Seeing two places set for dinner always reminded me how much I missed my father.

I missed Annie, too. She was the one person I could really talk to. Jean, on the other hand, was the no-fly zone when it came to discussing personal matters. She made everything worse. If she saw me all funky, she'd know something was wrong and want to talk about it. There was no way in the world I would ever mention anything important to Jean, especially Nigel McBride. She was clueless when it came to guys.

Actually, she was clueless about almost everything. She had no idea that I had my dad's stash. Or that I burned it as incense to have that feeling of him all around me. When Dad was having a dog day or the blues, he smoked hash. Just a little at a time, but often. He said it jump-started him out of the "no good thinking." I only hoped burning it all around me could do the same.

For the last two days, I had been burning bits and pieces. I even made a pipe out of a Tampax inserter. It was easy. I took the thick part of the cardboard tube and cut a small hole on the top at the end. Then I put a bit of tin foil in it. If I wanted to smoke hash, I could have dropped the little rock in it, lit up, cupped my palm over the end of it, and sucked it down. But after the vodka experiment, it didn't seem like a very good idea. So I used the pipe in the form of an altar. I kept it in my tent with a little picture of my dad. Burning his dope was like breathing the air he left behind.

My tent was like a beautiful cave until I started to smell my own B.O. and crawled out. The daylight hurt my eyes. I looked in the mirror. That's when I understood what people meant when they said that someone looked like "death warmed over." Something had to be done. After not showering or brushing for all that time, I smelled like cat food. I looked totally grody. That sucked. Girls shouldn't smell bad, even if they were dying. Actually there was a rule:

Always smell good.

I battled with the nylon shower curtain and eventually got myself situated under a stream of hot water. I lathered my body with Ivory soap and tried to wash my hair. Washing my hair was an event. When the hot water ran out, I knew it was clean.

I thought about how lucky I was to have gotten in with the locals at all. I may have messed it all up but, for a short time in my life, I had been in the epicenter of cool. Who really cared if I screwed up with Nigel McBride?

While conditioning my hair, I made some big decisions. I decided to ration the rest of my dad's stash so he'd stay with me a little longer. I'd eat everything Jean cooked then slide away into my tent until school started in September. I'd listen to every album I owned through my headphones and wait patiently.

I was naked and bent over drying my hair when Jean stormed into the bathroom. Even seeing her upside down, I could tell something was terribly wrong. She was chewing her necklace with the cross on it and shaking her head.

"Ever hear of knocking?" I asked flipping my hair back over my shoulder and twisting a towel around me.

She motioned me toward my room. As we made our way, she stepped on a pack of Red Vines and a day old Pop-Tart that was stuck in the carpeting just outside the tent. When she didn't scold me for using the floor as a garbage can, I knew it was serious.

"What?" I asked.

She clasped her hand over my mouth. Jesus Christ, were we getting robbed or something? Had aliens taken over Santa Monica? I was trying to get away but she grabbed my wrist hard like she used to when we crossed the volcanically active hillsides together on the big island.

"Do you know a boy named Nigel McBride?" she asked.

"What?" How did she know about Nigel?

Jean waited, egging me on with a smile. I nodded, thinking it was so weird to hear Nigel's name come out of her mouth. I wasn't about to get psyched out, but then she resealed my mouth with her hand.

"Do you?" she asked.

Was that a trick question or what?

She started hugging me in a way she hadn't since the Java Jones was sold, playing with my hair, and looking at me all funny. She giggled and tried to tickle me and then she really lost it. She jumped up and started dancing. She really cut loose, taking both of my hands and swinging me all around until we fell on top of my bed. Bummer, we banged against the tent. The needle on my turntable screeched across Joni Mitchell's tranquil voice, destroying *Blue*, one of my favorite albums of all time. Had Jean finally cracked?

"What's the matter with you?" I shouted.

Without a doubt, it was just like the night she got the news that Uncle Mike sold the Java Jones. Jean had had way too many tumblers of wine. I just wanted to know what the hell was up, but she kept goofing around. For a split second, I wondered what my life would be like if she actually went over the edge.

"Mom!"

Jean held my face in her hands and said, "Nigel McBride would like to have you over for dinner at his house tonight."

Before I could say anything, she continued, "With his parents, of course."

"What?" I asked again. "Did he call?"

"No. He's here."

Before she could start another sentence, I was jumping all over her, hopping into her arms, and twirling around like Julie Andrews in *The Sound of Music*. Then I stopped and stood there. Did she just say: Nigel McBride was here?

"He went to get his car," she said. Jean was in orbit because I was about to date one of the most eligible bachelors in the world. I knew she saw dollar signs instead of tan lines, but I didn't care. It felt so good to be happy with her.

"Get dressed," she said, dancing out of the room. "He'll be back any moment."

"Mom, please . . . be cool."

Cool was so far out of her range.

"Please," I said.

Ordinarily that comment would've caused a war between us, but this time Jean just closed her eyes for a beat and chilled on command. When she opened them, there was a strange look on her face. She whispered loudly after taking another sniff.

"Are you smoking Daddy's weed?"

"No, I'm just burning it for incense."

Jean took a look at the hash and whispered emphatically, "Honey, this is Daddy's happy stuff. You don't want to get high, do you?"

"No," I said.

"Well you will if you smell this long enough. Now get dressed." Jean picked up my incense tray, taking it with her as she left the room.

I ripped through my drawers looking for the perfect outfit. Nigel was due back any minute so I had no time to think. The only thing I knew for sure was that there was no way I'd blow it this time. Jesus gave me a second chance. This time I was going to nail it.

CHAPTER TWENTY

Girl Gospel

The first thing I did was put on my lucky underwear. I called them lucky because they left no panty lines and I never got my period in them. The rule:

Start at the bottom if you want perfection.

I also put on my fancy silk drawstring pants because I was meeting Nigel's parents. It was important to look casual but presentable, pretty but not prude.

Surfers like their girls super sweet, so I went for the rose pastel and white look. My shirt was lacy but not see-through. I wore clogs, five abalone bracelets, puka shell earrings, and a thin scarf made out of vintage Hawaiian fabric draped around my neck. I put primrose oil on my hair because Nigel liked that smell. My rabbit foot was tucked into the pocket of Annie's white jean jacket. The one with a puka shell sewn on for every guy she'd kissed. I had just gotten my lip gloss on when Jean slid into my room, all smiley and then not.

"You're not wearing that, are you?" she asked.

There was no way I was going to have a fashion war. I was too happy but I knew what Jean was thinking, the rules beyond the rules. Call it the bottom line. A kind of girl gospel that mothers drilled into their daughters. It went like this:

Girls must dress, act, and live a certain way for one reason. Boys won't like them if they don't. If a girl can't get a boyfriend, she'll never get a husband. A man completes a woman. You see, women are not even whole people until they get married. Every girl must save herself for that special day and then she'd live happily ever after. If a girl didn't follow these rules, before she knew it she'd be twenty-five, an old maid, and living with a cat. No friends or respect and no community to grow old in. She'd be alone forever like that Beatles song. She'd be Eleanor Rigby, die alone in some church, and get buried with her name.

Somehow what I was wearing boiled down to *all* that.

I prayed to Jesus and everybody else in the God category to help me get away from 33 Sage as quickly as humanly possible and to make Nigel fall in love with me once and for all.

"You're not wearing that," Jean said again. This time it was a statement, not a question.

"Mom," I mouthed, trying to get her to mellow.

"You are *not* going to the McBride home in those cheap Hawaiian clothes."

I could hear Nigel flipping through a magazine in the living room so arguing with Jean was not an option. I tried to reason with her and then I tried to bargain. I tried everything.

But Jean was being stubborn and wouldn't budge. She said, "Fine. Have it your way. I'll just tell him you won't be able to go."

Jean turned to leave the room. Before she could finish her sentence or get passed the doorframe, I slammed the door shut. There was no way she was going to ruin this for me. No way.

"Do you know who these people are?" she demanded. "They're in *LIFE* magazine this month with Billy Graham. They know the president of the United States. And they're richer than Uncle Mike will ever be."

I thought about tying Jean up, taping her mouth shut, and locking her in the closet. My hand clenched the door-knob as she paced around me. She stopped abruptly and started tapping her foot with her arms crossed.

"Do you want to be like me when you're thirty-two, struggling for every dime?" she asked.

"Hell no," I said.

"Then change your clothes."

"No," I said right to her face.

"Yes," Jean said. To make her point, she yanked my hair hard.

I pushed her. I didn't mean to slap my mother, it just happened. Before I could say I was sorry or ask her if she was okay, Jean pulled the door open, exposing both of us to Nigel. She straightened her patio dress and casually strolled down the hall as if nothing had happened. My hands were shaking, and I tasted blood in my mouth. Did she hit me or did I bite myself? I didn't have time to figure it out. Nigel was waiting. He was wearing baby blue cords, a white Hang Ten t-shirt, and Wallabees. He looked good in clothes and his dry hair had a slight wave. He was acting very polite and had a smile plastered on his face.

"What time would you like Nani home, Mrs. Nuuhiwa?" he asked.

"Midnight is my regular time," I said quickly, walking to him. "Right, Mom?"

Jean slowly opened the front door, pointed to her cheek, and waited until I kissed her. She took a step back and glared at me. That was the most pissed off I'd ever seen her in my whole life.

"You kids have fun," she chirped.

CHAPTER TWENTY-ONE

✻

Second Chance

I breathed a huge sigh of relief in Nigel's van and coughed. It smelled of Windex and a new piña colada air freshener that hung from the rearview mirror.

"I washed the van for you."

I didn't know what to say to that. There was nothing in the rules about when surfers do nice things or are super polite like Nigel was being.

The ocean was totally glassed off and the most righteous shade of blue I'd seen in Santa Monica. I never thought I'd appreciate a totally flat ocean as much as I did right then. The world was quiet without waves and smooth until Nigel cranked a tape in.

He shouted over the blown-out speakers, "I couldn't stop thinking about you."

That caught me completely off guard.

"This is my favorite song in the world," he went on. It was an eight-track of Norman Greenbaum's "Spirit in the Sky." I nodded along with the rhythm.

Then Nigel asked, "You want to know some of my other favorite things?" Of course I nodded yes. "My favorite strokes are freestyle and butterfly. I'm on the swim team at Harvard. That's my high school. It's just for guys. My favorite event is hundred butterfly. My favorite food after practice is two double patty cheeseburgers, fries, and an extra thick chocolate chip milkshake."

He went on telling me Twister was his favorite game. Pluto his favorite Disney character. He wanted to see the pyramids and Panama Canal. His least favorite subject was English, but he loved to read Hemingway. *What! What?* I yelled in my head. Guys, let alone surfers, back home didn't read. Not even comics. I nodded along with the music as Nigel continued to chat, pointing out important landmarks.

"You have to have fake ID or be over twenty-one to go up there. The Sunspot is like Roy's, locals only," Nigel said. "I use my older brother's driver's license."

Across from Temescal Beach, just off PCH, was a steep dirt road. At the top of it was a tiny art deco shack with a red neon light flashing SUNSPOT on and off. I made a memory photo in my mind.

Just before Topanga, Nigel showed me the haunted whorehouse.

"That's where Thelma Todd got murdered. She was a movie star in the thirties. I think her gangster boyfriend did it. The police found her dead in the garage." Nigel was a regular tour guide. He honked his horn.

"Hi Thelma," he waved. "Shawn and I used to sneak in there when we were younger. We'd hear weird noises all the time. And on the staircase it was so cold, we could see our breath even on hot days."

"Freak me out," I said.

"Freak me out," Nigel agreed. "We tried to catch feral cats. I love cats, but Shawn and I weren't allowed to have girly pets, only big dogs. Retrievers mostly, for hunting with my dad."

I was stunned how much he talked as we drove past the Chart House and Moonshadows. Annie made surfers sound like mutes, but this was not the case with Nigel McBride. He told me his whole life story.

We went past Malibu and Paradise Cove. When we got to Leo Carrillo, the beach had turquoise water like Hawaii. Nigel pulled over to the side of the road and told me, "This is where I talk to Jesus." He explained, "Since I accepted Christ, the ocean is my church and where I always feel God. He's almost like a liquid holy spirit, you know? It's like Jesus speaks to me through waves."

I nodded and said, "Totally."

This was the full-on date. I was going to meet his parents. I had to ace this. We had been driving for like forty-five minutes. Norman Greenbaum had been replaced by Jethro Tull.

"Did you know Tull is born-again?" Nigel asked.

"Cool," I said.

There were horses running free on the lush hillsides and a few stables scattered behind an endless white picket fence.

"It's really beautiful up here."

The sound of my voice surprised me; it was hashed-out and calm even though inside I was like a jumping bean.

I guess Jean was right about secondhand smoke because I really sounded mellow. Nigel smiled and softly put his hand on my face, gently turning my head toward a sign that had a "W" spray-painted over Cortez Beach.

"That's where I buried Wiggles my hamster. My dad doesn't go for sentimental stuff. Fish are flushed, burial at sea, and all other pets are bagged and tossed into the trash. But Wiggles got a real burial. I put him in one of those long matchboxes, dug a little hole by that sign, and made a cross out of eucalyptus leaves. Dad never noticed. He's only into golf and guns. That 'W' stands for Wiggles. We renamed this place Wiggles Beach."

Nestled just beyond a row of trees was an ornate iron fence with a giant "M" on it.

"There's my house," he said.

Talk about the pearly gates. I'd never seen anything so fancy. My back was sweating, and I needed a smoke. Then my stomach started to growl. I was trying not to fidget, but the gurgling was out of control. Two important rules came into play:

Never fidget.
Never let them see you panic.

It wasn't even five yet, but I hoped there would be some rolls or snacks before dinner that would help quiet down my stomach.

The fact that Nigel wasn't very good at driving a stick was definitely making the situation worse. Every time he shifted, I was thrown forward and then slammed back. By the time we pulled into the driveway, I felt carsick.

"What's the secret password, mate?" Lord Ricky said, springing out from behind a large banana shrub. I jumped so high I almost went through the sunroof.

"Jeez, Rick!" Nigel yelled.

Lord Ricky was wearing a neck brace and a kid's pirate hat. He had a patch over one eye and a plastic hook dangling from his left arm. His lieutenants were wearing trunks and jackets but no shirts. Were they invited for dinner, too?

"You asked me to watch the front gate," Lord Ricky said, poking at my window like I was a fish in a bowl. I rolled it down and asked, "What happened to you?"

Like I cared.

Lord Ricky explained he ate it at The Wedge down in Newport. He sprained his neck but didn't get paralyzed. Nigel continued, "He did a total rag doll when he hit the bottom because he was so loaded."

Lord Ricky held up his beer and saluted. He said, "Pardy Hardy."

Brad and Stu were smoking cigars, which didn't help my stomach one bit. I could hear dogs barking and music playing somewhere down the driveway. I looked around and saw a few dozen vans and tons of cars parked on Pacific Coast Highway. Nigel was laughing as Lord Ricky did a little jig and pushed open the gate. With the motor idling and radio turned off, I could hear metal clanging in the back and realized the van was filled with kegs of beer. There must have been ten of them stacked on top of each other.

"Just keep Valley Dudes out," Nigel said over his shoulder as he downshifted then put his hand on my leg.

The driveway leading to Nigel's house was long and curvy. In the distance, I could see a large pink hacienda-style estate with a red terra-cotta tiled roof. It was the most beautiful home I'd ever seen.

"That's the guesthouse," Nigel said, pointing. It reminded me of the Kahala Gardens where I used to watch rich Japanese girls from Punahou get married. This place made Uncle Mike's home look like a low-rent apartment on Hotel Street.

I wanted to disappear. It would be perfect, I thought, if I could just twitch my nose from side to side, blink a couple of times, and *poof,* be gone. Nigel drove us around a turnabout and down another steep driveway. I noticed a sign marked SERVICE ENTRANCE.

I wondered how everyone got down this monster driveway. The music was louder and louder the closer we got. Then I saw rows of golf carts with MCBRIDE written in bold navy blue letters on either side. I felt like such a stoner. Everything was moving slow. Nigel blasted his horn as we made a final turn and that's when I saw the crowd. There must have been more than two hundred people there, cheering and clapping their hands. A band was playing. Nigel asked me, "Do you like Honk?"

Not only did I like Honk, I had a Honk t-shirt.

"They're hot," I said.

Honk's music was like one perfect wave after another. They were legendary in Southern California. The band scored the soundtrack for *Five Summer Stories*. It was being called the best surfing film since *Endless Summer*. Gerry Lopez was in it, too. I'd almost forgotten about Gerry Lopez.

"The band came up from Corona del Mar when they heard we were having a party. But once they got here and started playing, I realized it wouldn't be a party without you," Nigel said and kissed me in front of everyone.

I laid my head on Nigel's shoulder as we drove toward a kidney-shaped pool. A hoard of people, including Jerry and Shawn, swarmed the van. I could see the Lisas, Mary Jo, Suzie, and Jenni, sunning on lounges while Rox and Claire floated in the pool on queen-sized rafts. Everyone else was into the music. Guys were dancing, pogo-ing up and down as the voice of Honk's lead singer, Steve Wood, echoed through the property.

Shawn guided Nigel into a parking spot close to a cabana and an outside dining area. The main estate was on a hill behind us. It was nothing short of spectacular. It looked like a postcard I had seen of The Beverly Hills Hotel.

All of State Beach was there.

"Is that Bob, the lifeguard?" I asked.

"Yeah," Nigel said. He wasn't very excited about seeing him. "If we get him laid once in a while, we get more waves."

That made sense to me, but I wondered which chick would actually sacrifice herself to that dweeb. When I looked around, something dawned on me. Everyone was in bathing suits. Even Nigel had dropped his pants and unbuttoned his shirt. But not me, oh no, I was TCFS, too cool for school, in my dinner-with-Nigel's-parents outfit. What a hash-head I was. I had broken the oldest rule in the book:

Never go anywhere without a bathing suit.

There was no way I'd make it through the night without a suit. I couldn't even take off my clogs because my silky draw-string pants weren't hemmed and I'd be tripping all over them. I tied up my blouse and rolled it back so my midriff was totally exposed. I looked very Bianca Jagger standing by her private jet. Then, I decided to roll my pants down on my hips. This sexy-ass look with my scarf tied around my wrist to hide the extra jewelry I wore to impress Mr. and Mrs. McBride would become my signature look. I actually had created my very own State style, just like Claire was the only one who wore turquoise and Rox was the only one who wore far out necklaces and bathing suit tops instead of shirts. I would always be known for low pants and a tied-up blouse.

One of the little Mar Vista skateboarders whizzed by me and somersaulted into the pool, skateboard and all. When he sprung up, he shouted my way, "You're a fox."

Nigel flipped him off.

He flipped Nigel off.

All was well.

Smelling hash made me brave. I felt good. It was like I was in my dad's mind. The Jimmy Star groove. Clean, cool, and confident. Smelling Dad's hash made me feel like I'd never have to say goodbye and in a weird way it was like he was still with me, in the background cheering me on. The party was beyond bitchin'.

III

'Awkake

August 1972

Virgo

♍

CHAPTER TWENTY-TWO

✳

Christmas in July

I was the only one who wasn't in the pool. At least I didn't have to meet Nigel's folks. Mr. McBride was in Texas with his old hunting buddy, the coach of the Dallas Cowboys, and Mrs. McBride was up in Santa Barbara with her staff, planning a fundraiser for The Crippled Children's Society. In other words, the place was ours.

Word had gotten out that there was a party at the McBride's. People showed up from everywhere. Nigel pointed out guys he called Weird Wayne, Snap, and Dominator. These weren't just *haoles* with cute nicknames in Birdie trunks. They were living, breathing photo layouts from *Surfer* magazine. Of course, they weren't alone: following them at a respectful distance were Miss Weird Wayne, Miss Snap, and Miss Dominator.

Only the escorted and babes-in-training got past Lord Ricky at the gate. Once inside, girl games were in full swing. The sun hadn't set yet, but the place was already maxed out. It was going to be a huge night that separated the real Honeys from the wannabes.

With so many goddesses in a closed off area, the smart move was to stay with my own pack. The lineup was all smiles when I walked over. I ranked right up there at the top after driving in with Nigel. I was as good as in with everyone now, except for Rox. Something just wasn't right with her; she was so uptight.

But Claire was loving me. While the kegs were being set up, she showed off her hostess skills by opening giant bags of Doritos, Fritos, and pretzels then dumping them into bowls. As I walked by, she stopped and took me aside.

She leaned in and spoke confidentially, "Nigel is totally in love with you."

I blushed.

"You're so cute, Nani," Claire said as she wrapped her arms around me. I lay my head on her chest and took a deep whiff of her Avon Lady Charisma perfume. For that moment, everything in the world was perfect until my stomach growled.

"Was that you?" Claire asked.

I buried my face in my hands. I was so embarrassed.

"Well, do something about it, quick," she insisted and turned away.

Mary Jo came to my rescue. She handed me a beer to wash some pretzels down. Somehow that combination was supposed to settle my insides. I took the plastic cup of beer as a peace offering, raised it up, and made a toast.

"To friends."

"To friends," she said happily.

I wanted just a sip, but Mary Jo held onto the bottom of the cup so I had to keep drinking. She wouldn't let go until all the beer was gone.

"Okay?" I asked.

"Yeah," she said, still smiling.

"I'm really sorry about what happened. It's been kind of weird lately."

"Bygones," she said and waltzed into the crowd.

On an empty stomach that beer hit me right between the eyes.

Nigel strolled back over, holding a giant slice of pepperoni pizza.

"Hungry?" he asked.

I was starving and it smelled so good, but I shook my head from side to side. A rule's a rule. No eating around guys.

"Good, I wanna show you something."

He grabbed a six-pack, took my hand, and started running. With clogs on, it was hard to keep up with him. He stopped and gave me a piggyback ride. We galloped along what seemed like football fields of perfect rose beds. There were these hedges on each side of the path, two tennis courts, more flowers than I had ever seen in one place, and a line of giant cypress trees marking the property line. Finally, we stopped at a small cement building. "This is the fort," he said.

The fort overlooked the Pacific, which was flat as a pancake. It must have been at least a three-hundred-foot drop to the sand. No waves, no surfing, which meant the party could go on for days. I slid off Nigel's back while he turned the combination of a padlock on the front door. There were snorkels, fins, and wet suits hanging on a clothesline drying out.

"03-06-55 . . . that's my birthday," he said.

I'd never forget those numbers. March the sixth made Nigel McBride a Pisces. That meant he was trusting, spiritual, and a bit slippery. Not easy to catch. Not easy to hold on to.

"Only me, you, and Shawn know that combo."

He pushed against the steel plate door. It sounded like fingernails scratching a chalkboard. It was pitch black inside and as cold as a meat locker. But, like a full-on gentleman, Nigel took my hand and led me down a bunch of stairs.

"There's a light in here somewhere," he said, leaning over me and lifting my chin with one hand. His skin was moist and his breath was hot and smelled like mozzarella cheese. I could feel him coming closer. Then, in total darkness, he kissed my eyeball.

"Okay, onward," he said, returning to his search.

Patting the wall with the palm of his hand, he began whistling "Layla" by Derek and the Dominos. I told him that I loved that song even though I had only heard it once.

"Ah, here it is," he said.

The room lit up in a flash.

Tiny red and green lights intertwined with tinsel blinked on all around us. There were Styrofoam snowflakes on the walls and plastic reindeer on the floor. It was kind of romantic.

"My grandfather built this as a bomb shelter during World War II," Nigel said as he moved aside cardboard boxes marked FRAGILE with the side of his foot. "But as you can see, it's a storage room now."

This was the notorious fort that every girl dreamed about? From the way Claire and Rox talked, it sounded like a castle, not a dump yard for holiday decorations. I wondered if there was another room hidden behind a door or something.

During the holidays, Jean always decorated the Java Jones. It drove my dad crazy. She'd put Santa hats on the mounted pufferfish that hung over the bar and make me and the hostesses wear muumuus with the words MELE KALIKIMAKA and MERRY CHRISTMAS written on them. We didn't have a chimney, but every year Santa left me chocolate-covered macadamia nuts and toys in my stocking. But nothing Jean did had ever come close to what was going on here.

Nigel explained that his mother was famous for her decorations and that it took two trucks to move all the ornaments into their main house in Hancock Park. All I heard were the words "main house."

"This isn't where you live?" I said, immediately sorry for asking such a stupid question. Why did I have to talk so much? Naturally, there was a rule:

Guys like to be listened to, not talked to.

Nigel played with my hair, scooping it into his arms like water, and bumped his hip into mine. He was patient as he explained that this house was used for holiday parties, political fundraisers, and garden club meetings. He made a point to let me know that he and Shawn stayed out here during the summers.

As he talked, he pushed aside boxes to make a place for us to sit on the floor. He made me feel special. Nigel was so cute. He had the sweetest grin on his face when he handed me a box marked BROKEN.

"What's this?" I asked.

"Guess."

Nigel didn't wait for an answer. He was excited like a little boy with an unopened present. Inside was a giant Tupperware bowl like the ones my mom used to keep fruit salad in. Nigel popped open the lid to show me hundreds of buds, and I'm not talking rosebuds. He said it was his secret stash. This was big time. Guys just didn't do this. He may as well have asked me to marry him or hold his surfboard, showing off his stash was *that* special. It smelled homegrown, but I didn't dare ask him something that personal yet.

Nigel pulled a bamboo bong out from under an elf's red fleece pants. I smiled, watching him perform surgery on each little hole of the bong bowl, removing hash resin with a toothpick, but not spilling the stinky bong water.

"I made this in shop class," he said.

I wondered if Nigel was expecting me to smoke with him or maybe get into touchy feely stuff below the belt. Screwing was out. Any girl who did that stuff with a guy who wasn't her full-on boyfriend got the reputation of being a slut. And I didn't want to end up like Suzie, who really blew it, if you catch my drift. My heart was pounding when I thought of the unbreakable rule:

No sex.

Nigel looked directly in my eyes as he lit the bong. He drew a long, hard hit, making the water in the bottom bubble loudly.

"Hey," he said.

"Hey," I said back.

Nigel looked instantly high. His face was magenta, his body went all rubbery, and his eyelids got heavy. He handed me the bong and slowly exhaled an endless stream of smoke into my face.

"Whoa," Nigel groaned.

He curled up and laid his head in my lap. He looked up at me with droopy blue eyes. It was my turn. I had seen Dad do this a thousand times. How hard could it be? I tried to look cute as I sucked what was left in the bowl. The pot felt like tickling powder in my lungs and corn kernels popping out of my head. I thought my skull would split wide open. This was the kind of bud my dad would have called *primo*. I had to hand it to Dad for being able to smoke this stuff first thing every morning and still function all day. I was fried after one hit but didn't cough.

I tried to prop myself up, but I felt like I was melting. Someone who sounded like me was laughing somewhere in the room. My eyes were squeezed shut and tears were rolling down my face. The closer Nigel got, the harder I laughed. He was sprawled out on top of me, biting my neck while he tried to untangle ornaments that had gotten wrapped around my ankles like seaweed all knotted up on the ocean floor. He poked my ribs and tickled me under my shirt. My hair was everywhere. I was laughing so hard I almost peed.

Then Nigel took off his shirt and things got totally quiet. Too quiet. But I actually felt more comfortable with Nigel with his shirt off. He looked familiar, and I got a tingle when his skin touched mine. It was just our shoulders, but everything was electric until he took a giant gulp of beer, burped, then leaned in and kissed me. I cringed, but then I thought about how Nigel McBride looked in the ocean, all liquid and Jesus-like, barreling into a wave.

He wiped his mouth and handed me the rest of the beer. I pretended to drink his backwash, no problem. He lay down next to me so stoned I thought he was going to fall asleep.

"You're gnarly, Nani," Nigel said, all stoked, but with his eyes still closed.

He reached up, searching for me with his hands, and gently pulled me down to his face. We kissed again for a long time. His tongue darted in and out of my mouth. We rolled around on the floor until a stack of boxes fell on top of us. Luckily it was only wrapping paper, not glass ornaments. We stood up and started laughing again. Nigel leaned me against the plastic reindeer. Then he backed up very slowly and told me with great concern, "Wait. Here."

I watched Nigel spread out a red tree skirt on the floor. THE McBRIDE FAMILY was embroidered in gold thread. He tossed a long green banner over it and pulled down the cover like a bedspread. Then he sprayed Cedar Enhancement from something like a hairspray bottle to get rid of the moldy smell. I tried not to panic. Did he think we were going to do it? I wondered if I should tell him I was a virgin, but that was lame. We lay down next to each other. He rolled me over onto my back, and I screamed. Hanging from the rafters just above me was a giant glow-in-the-dark Santa Claus.

Nigel thought I was so funny. "Santa likes to watch," he giggled and started kissing me again. I tried to look sexy and Barbarella-ish, but it was hard. Making out this intensely took a lot of concentration. It was sort of like rubbing my stomach and patting my head at the same time. How the heck did any girl look good doing this? We kept getting twisted in my hair and once or twice he had to totally reposition me. But things were going smoothly until my stomach growled really loud. Nigel sat up and touched my belly button.

"Was that you?" he asked, talking to my stomach like it was a person or something. He patted it gently and placed his ear to it and said, "I'm trying to see if we can get K Earth 101. Oh man, you got a storm in there."

He tore open a candy cane wrapper with his teeth and stuck half of it in my mouth. The peppermint tasted a thousand years old but I didn't care. I'd never been so embarrassed in my entire life. I had to distract him. I started to kiss him again, but this time he pulled away. I held my stomach, forcing it to be silent.

"You know what, Nani? You should be my girlfriend," he blurted out.

Oh my God. Wait until Claire and Rox hear about this. Better yet, wait 'til Jean finds out I'm going steady with Nigel McBride. This was better than becoming Little Miss Aloha or winning the Hawaiian Village Hula Contest. I smiled because everything was going to be alright. I was going to be Nigel McBride's girlfriend. There was absolutely nothing to worry about. Every rule was covered now.

"Yeah, that would be cool," I said.

He dug into his pocket and pulled out an aqua blue Saint Christopher medal and fastened the necklace around my neck. "I really like you," he said, playing with my hair. "You're my girlfriend now, right?"

I felt a giant gurgle starting to erupt from my stomach. As it growled, I kissed him full-on. I had to do something to distract Nigel from the sound. Then I covered up the noise by saying, "Oh, oh." Nigel took that as some kind of girl sign and kissed me more.

The more noise I made close to his ears, the more turned on he got. Every time a growl, gurgle, or rumble rolled out of my stomach, I moaned a bit louder. I moaned so loud, we couldn't hear the band in the distance. I felt kind of silly and to stop myself from laughing again, I had to think of something sad like the way Oahu looked from the window in the airplane, disappearing into the sea.

We weren't doing it, but the way we moved and touched with our clothes on sure made Nigel sweat up a storm. I felt like I was in a double class of PE. It just went on and on. I was getting tired. I tried to imagine what people were doing at the party. Suddenly Nigel got all stiff and still, and just like that it was over.

I tried to sit up, but he got all lovey dovey with me. He curled in really close, held my hands, and stared deep into my eyes. I told myself to look happy even though I was feeling claustrophobic and creeped out by the Santa's glowing eyes above us and his wide plastic grin.

"I love you, Nani," Nigel said.

I was so tired. I wanted to say: you taste like bong juice and make-out sessions are totally overrated. If you weren't a surfer and pretty as a girl with long blonde hair, I'd probably never do this again.

But instead I said, "Love you too."

CHAPTER TWENTY-THREE

Dancing Poodles

I was glad to be out of Santa's make-out dungeon. The sun was setting, and there was a strong, warm breeze. Nigel told me the winds were called Santa Anas. I liked the idea of wind having a name. The whole sky was changing, and it felt like I was being swallowed by the color pink. My skin felt prickly and electric. I wondered how women could screw every night, and even in the mornings. Is that what marriage was all about? Pleasing your man? Having a baby, driving carpool, and getting a hobby?

Nigel and I walked back to the party hand in hand. I deliberately stepped on pockets of Mrs. McBride's blue pansies. I know this sounds weird, but it looked like they were laughing at me. They had tiny shaking stems with leaves that pinched my ankles when I kicked through them. The kumquats in the trees lining the tennis courts were turning toward us when we strolled by even though the wind was blowing in the opposite direction.

My hair smelled like mildew and the cedar spray. I was starting to feel funky. Then I remembered another rule:

Never look angry.

I thought of the happy face sticker. A yellow circle with two dots for eyes and a U-shaped smile. All I had to do was put on a happy face and stroll back into the party.

Claire raised her eyebrows when she saw us. Nigel and I crunched through the crowd toward the lineup. Honk was getting a standing ovation. Girls were squealing and guys were spiraling up, clapping their hands. The place was packed shoulder to shoulder with blondes. Claire yelled over the music to Rox, "Does she smell like cedar to you?"

Rox zoned in on me and sniffed, "Have you been in the fort?"

The Lisas winked and Suzie slid a beer into my hands.

"No hard feelings," she said.

I was just about ready to tell her I wasn't thirsty when Rox grabbed the beer.

Suzie looked like she was going to have a hissy fit when Rox put the drink to her mouth and started to chugalug. At the same time, Mary Jo ran past her. It looked like she deliberately plowed into Rox. The beer went flying into Claire's hair, and if I hadn't been standing so close to the edge of the pool and grabbed Rox, she would have fallen in. Rox was furious. No one ever grabbed or bumped her.

Mary Jo turned back and said, "Oops, sorry."

Rox mimicked, "Oops, sorry," and pushed her into the pool.

That triggered a few other jumpers doing cannon balls.

"Has Mary Jo gone mental?" Claire asked Suzie.

Annie Iopa would be so proud of how well I was doing. But she had warned me that after I scored, it would be all about maintaining my status. How hard could that be,

I wondered, looking up at Nigel. He was still grinning ear to ear. I had this thing licked. There were no more worries. It was time to enjoy myself. Finally I could relax.

Miss Dominator gave Nigel and me "the nod." So did all the girls in her lineup. It was totally surreal. The chicks were saying hello to me before they said hello to Nigel. They looked so cool in their white Landlubber bell-bottoms, Bernardo sandals, and halter tops.

Rox broke the spell. She was standing behind me. Before I could spin around and say a word to her, she turned to Nigel and said, "Can we please borrow Nani?" in her best little girl voice.

"Just for a minute," Nigel said, carving a path through the crowd.

The Lisas linked their arms around me. We weaved through what seemed like miles of saffron surfers with bare chests. They were scoping all their options, picking their date for the night. Of course the Lisas were getting the most attention from the wave-starved troops. They were wearing strapless tops and embroidered Levi shorts with moccasin boots. I don't know why they decided to dress the same that night, but it was really working for them.

Mary Jo dragged herself out of the pool as we walked by. She looked like a wet mop in her jeans and ruined leather sandals. Suzie lugged her up the driveway, and they disappeared together.

"That's weird," Claire said, watching them leave. "When did they become best buds?"

I didn't have a clue what was going on. Nigel, Shawn, and Jerry joined KC and a bunch of hard-core Redondo Beach types who were arm wrestling and drinking tequila after they lit it on fire. Those babies were called Flamers. They must have been very powerful because the fire seemed to suspend in midair in front of KC's mouth as she kicked one back then slammed her elbow onto the bar to leverage herself into a position of total dominance. A guy grabbed her hand and their upper arms locked. It took her one second to break his grip. She was so focused, her opponent never had a chance. It looked like a trail of crystal blue light hung in front of her mouth.

"Do you see that?" I asked Rox.

"Yeah, KC's got super strength. She doesn't bleed," Rox said, pushing me to the cabana.

In the dark, just for a moment, it looked like she was smiling, but just with her eyes.

"Thanks for saving my ass back there," Rox said, nudging me forward as we cut the long line of girls waiting for the bathroom.

Claire, Jenni, and the Lisas followed. We were all jammed into the tiny bathroom. It had dark gray wallpaper with the words *bonjour* and *je t'aime* written in fancy white script. Sometimes it looked like the words were moving and the pink poodles on the wallpaper were wagging their tails. Everybody was too busy taking turns peeing and asking what happened with Nigel to notice the wallpaper was alive, breathing in and out.

I was not going to lose my mind at the McBrides' in front of Rox and Claire. No way, José. I closed my eyes to focus, center my mind, and chill. No one in that powder room was going to know something was wrong unless I told them.

At that moment, I thought, there should be a rule:

No bong balls.

Rox kept asking, "Did you or didn't you go all the way?"

She grilled me like Perry Mason. She was being awful and wouldn't stop. I looked at her all innocent-like. Why not? I was innocent. I didn't go all the way. I looked those goon girls in the eye and told every one of them the truth, "For the hundredth time," I said. "We didn't do it."

The lineup watched my every move like some kind of girl jury. Claire was brushing the beer out of her hair and rubbing cinnamon potpourri in it to get rid of the smell. Rox tossed her cigarette in the sink and soaked the butt before she flicked it into the trash.

"What did you do with him?" She was fuming.

I didn't know how to answer. Rox smiled when I hesitated. She knew she had me on that one.

"We had a major make-out session," I told her.

Claire was beaming like I was a saint or something.

"Making out is okay," she said hugging and kissing me.

"So you didn't go all the way?" Rox asked just to be sure.

I couldn't believe what I was seeing. The poodles were dancing off the walls and onto Rox's head. I told them, "Stop it."

"No," Rox said to me.

She was so pissed off, kind of like my mom was before I left tonight. Rox's face was getting blotchy. She dug into the velvet shorts she had put on for evening wear. That was not easy considering they were so tight they looked like they had been painted on. Somehow she got her hand into the back pocket, pulled out a ten-dollar bill, and slapped it into Claire's hand.

"Don't gloat," Rox said.

"I knew you were a good girl," Claire whispered in my ear.

She was still hugging me as Jenni and the Lisas patted me on the back approvingly and squeezed their way out of the bathroom. There was a bet? That sucked.

Claire was so happy, admiring us in the mirror, comparing our Saint Christopher necklaces. The words *protect us* circled the image of Saint Christopher dodging lightning bolts on both our medals but my casing was deeper than hers. It made mine more special.

"Now we're like sisters-in-law," she said and hugged me goodbye.

In the mirror I could see Rox leaning against the towel rack, glaring at me. No more smiles. She bent over the sink. I shrugged my shoulders and stepped over the little pink poodles on the floor. Rox pounced forward and blocked the door with her arm.

"You stay right there," she demanded. Her face was right in mine, and the back of my head bumped into the light switch. The room went dark and wouldn't you know it, the poodles on the wallpaper glowed. How could the lineup just leave me with this Scorpio? That sign hated to lose or feel one-upped. I had to do something. Rox was moving in for the kill.

"What's that?" I asked, pointing to Rox's chin. Even in the dark I could see her head drop, looking down.

Before she could answer, I flipped up my finger and tweaked the tip of her nose. A soft orange light trailed behind my hand. I ducked under her arm and said, "Later gator."

I made a mad dash, turned the corner into the dressing room, and slammed into an enormous woman. She looked like a Bavarian elk hunter I had seen in *National Geographic*. Her braided blonde hair was piled high on her head. She had painted brown eyebrows, round, rosy cheeks, and glasses perched on the bridge of her turned-up nose. Her chin jiggled when she moved and her beady blue eyes matched a vest with giant brass buttons protruding over her breasts, which shot forward like two cannons. She wobbled in bedroom slippers with fur on them, holding a brandy snifter and cigarette in one hand and a slice of pizza in the other.

Rox tapped my shoulder and politely moved me to one side as she said, "Hello, Mrs. McBride."

Mrs. McBride asked Rox, "How are your parents, dear?" It sounded like one word the way she slurred it.

I thought everyone knew Rox's folks were dead. How could Mrs. McBride ask such a question? Didn't she know who Rox was?

I looked at Rox. She looked at me. Then we both looked back at Mrs. McBride.

"They're fine, thank you," Rox said.

"Well, give them my best," said Mrs. McBride, opening the cabana's sliding glass door.

I stuck my tongue in the space between my front teeth and waited. Rox was resealing her invisible armor. I couldn't tell if she was going to laugh or cry. Mrs. McBride made her way through the crowd outside, turning on the pool light as she left.

Rox jostled her boobs into a more perfect alignment. Then she pointed at my chest and said, "Are you cold?"

I thought to myself, *I'm always cold.* I had to get my jacket. It had my lucky rabbit foot in it and I needed its mojo fast. I remembered I left it in the fort.

"Now what?" she asked.

"I've got to jam to the fort."

"Well, you won't get in." Rox told me. "It's always locked."

"It's okay, I know the combo."

"You know the combo?"

It looked like a flashbulb went off in Rox's face, temporarily blinding her. I could almost hear the sizzle and pop. She stood motionless, waxy and overexposed, her chestnut hair blowing off her face and her mouth pursed tight. She was stunned.

Right then, I could have died happy.

CHAPTER TWENTY-FOUR

Saved

I wasn't exactly sure how I got there, but I was on a patio table dancing a very nasty hula. The music roared out of giant speakers right into my back. Rod Stewart was singing, "I'm Losing You." Bright lights shone under the thick glass of the table, illuminating every move I made. The whole party was cheering except Rox. She was clapping her hands, but she wasn't into the music. Nigel swung his shirt over his head like a cowboy about to rope a steer while Shawn and Jerry jumped up and down to the long drum solo. I concentrated on staying in the groove and tried to figure out how long I had been dancing.

The music was getting faster and faster. The guys went wild every time I made a motion with my hips. They hollered like they were getting tubed in the biggest wave ever. I arched my back and pushed my hips out toward the crowd but I kept an eye on Nigel. That was law now that I was wearing his Saint Christopher.

In Hawaii, I was not very good at hula. I remembered how my teacher Miss Kekahuna used to watch me through thick glasses and click her tongue at how stiff I was. I wasn't stiff now. Miss Kekahuna used her big arms to demonstrate, but I could never get my hands and feet moving together at the same time. I'd chant, pray for purification, and wear shapeless red linen dresses to honor Pele, but I couldn't hula. Miss Kekahuna would remind me, "Roll back on your feet, keep the shoulders leveled, elbows bent, and never slide. Always keep your steps tiny and close to the ground."

Now, on top of the table at Nigel's party, I could hula big time—left and right. If Miss Kekahuna could have seen me I probably would've won a trophy or something.

The drum solo was coming to an end. Rod Stewart's voice crackled in the warm night air. The Lisas were dancing hard, lunging forward and dipping back. Nag Champa incense was burning. That meant the Topanga Girls and more pot had arrived. But at that moment, standing on that table, I was the center of the universe. Like Anita Pallenberg in the Secret Chamber of Dreams, smoking a giant hookah and tasting the essence of man, I understood everything.

Nigel grabbed me by the thighs and lifted me up. It reminded me of tandem surfing with my father in Waikiki when I was still small enough to be carried. I was sailing through the air like I used to, up in the sky, safe and happy again. Nigel hoisted me over his shoulder as if I were a cavewoman. My hair touched his ankles as he scooted me away behind the tennis courts. I could hear the ocean in front of us and the party behind us. I imagined his Neanderthal knuckles dragging on the ground and the smell of bones around his neck. Strands of hair flew in and out of my mouth, and my stomach started to growl again. I wished I had eaten some of that ham Jean cooked.

My stomach was so close to his ear there was no way I could hide it this time. It sounded like the *Titanic* sinking.

"Tummy." Nigel said, looking directly at my belly button.

I was getting used to him talking to my stomach like it was a two-year-old.

"Don't you ever eat?"

Before I could answer, he put me down on the lawn and ran off, yelling back to me, "I'm going to get you something really tasty. Wait right there."

It was pitch black in front of me. The tennis court floodlights started to spin around like when I did too many cartwheels in a circle. I tried to walk but my knees were too rubbery. I decided to lie down and look up at the sky, searching through the stars and trying to remember which zodiac sign went where.

When I opened them again, Nigel was on top of me. It felt like all bets were off. We were kissing in the middle of the lawn and my funny bone had slammed into a sprinkler head. My elbow hurt so much. I thought about poor old Tinkerbell slipping and plowing her elbow into the cement the day World War III almost broke out at State.

"Where's my jacket?" I asked. I needed my lucky rabbit foot. Things were getting weird.

Nigel's tongue went deep in my ear and his hand went up my shirt. He suddenly stopped what he was doing.

"I don't know where your jacket is," he said.

He stared at me for a second, smiled, and flipped my hair side to side.

"I always wanted to do that," he said without taking a breath.

I didn't know what time it was. Nothing made any sense. If I wasn't home by midnight, Jean would go crazy. And where the hell was my jacket?

"The fort," I exclaimed. That's where I was going.

Nigel looked puzzled, but I guess he was just really stoned, too. He lay in the middle of the lawn with his hands behind his head, staring at the stars. When I tried to get up, he pulled me down and started to kiss me again. It was too rough. Then a sharp metal wire pricked my tongue. I jerked away when I tasted blood in my mouth.

Nigel said, "You wanna see my retainer?" He flicked it out of his mouth. There was a front tooth attached.

That's when it hit me.

"Shawn!" I shouted.

Shawn put a finger to my lips and broke out laughing. He laughed so hard he snorted and kind of spit. It was like Rox said: Shawn and Claire were the perfect couple. Neither one of them had all their teeth. I didn't think it was funny. I was in big trouble all around. If Claire or Nigel found out about *this* make-out session, my ass would be grass. I'd be labeled a slut, a flirt, or worse, people would start calling me Suzie.

Shawn was the playboy, not Nigel. Who knew how many girls he had snagged by pretending to be his brother? He was the one giving Nigel the stud reputation. It was diabolical and there was no way I could confront him because it was taboo to come between the brother bond. And if I told

Claire I would be busting myself. Shawn had this totally wired. Then it dawned on me. Poor Suzie, she actually did it with him.

"Shawn, swear to God you won't tell," I demanded.

Shawn looked bowled over. He flattened his hair with both hands and tugged at his trunks, straightening himself out. He was thinking again, and I knew this could take a while. Trying hard to maintain balance, I waited for his answer. Finally, he stood up and said, "As Jesus is my Lord and Savior . . ." he crossed his heart and said, "I swear."

I had forgotten the Christian thing. What a stroke of luck. I put him right back in church and nailed him with the God card. For once, I had actually nipped something in the bud.

I had to find a way to let him off the hook before he left. Guys couldn't lose face and if they did, they hated you for it. If I didn't say something nice, he'd think I was a bitch. Girls always had to be nice. What a royal pain in the ass. It was a rule:

Be nice, no matter what.

"Shawn," I said, as he walked away.

My mind was empty and I needed to think fast. I tried not to freak out when the grass started marching out of the lawn in a double row. "Oh Christ," I said. It just popped out.

Shawn stopped and turned back to look at me. I remembered what happened to Tinkerbell when she used the name of the Lord in vain in front of Nigel. Obviously, Shawn felt the same. By the way his lips curled, I could tell he was about to say something really mean. I saw it coming.

"Oh Christ, thank you." I blurted out before he could say a word, then I added, "Let's pray."

I took Shawn's hands into mine and performed the best imitation of my mother I could muster up. I remembered the way she talked to Jesus when she stood over my father's coffin. Her pleading voice softened as she said his name.

"Jesus," I said, looking down at Shawn's bare feet. "Thank you for giving Shawn McBride the courage and faith to honor you and not his earthly desires. May I return his strength with respect and kindness. Thank you, Lord. Amen."

"Amen," Shawn said while gently squeezing my hands.

What a cheeto jerk I was. That little act would probably send me to hell. But for the moment, in Shawn's eyes, I was a righteous, Jesus-loving girl who had been saved by the Lord like all Hawaiian savages ought to be.

CHAPTER TWENTY-FIVE

Ambushed

Thirty miles wasn't that far to walk. That's what I told myself as I looked for the way out of the estate. I wasn't going to get any crazier around Nigel or his jerk brother. Girlfriend or not, I was taking matters into my own hands.

The cars on the long, sloping driveway were parked fender to fender like at a drive-in movie. I followed the dense planting, hoping it would take me to the highway. There was a strong smell of exhaust and rubber. The moon was almost full in the highest part of the sky.

"Midnight," I shouted.

"Tick-tock," Lord Ricky chimed in. "Got to be somewhere, Cinderella?"

Lord Ricky sat in his station wagon parked next to Nigel's van. Both cars were blocking the main gate. On PCH, crowds of people huddled together, sneaking in one at a time.

"Aren't you supposed to be watching the entrance?"

Lord Ricky said nothing. Instead he blew smoke rings up into my face. Two girls sitting in the front seat giggled. They looked about eleven. Lord Ricky gave me a sidelong glance.

He looked like a troll trying to twist his head with his neck brace on and kiss one of the girls. He couldn't quite get into position. He was gross. Totally gross.

I zigzagged off the path. It was hard to walk with only one clog on and easy to trip. I fell over a thick garden hose into a shrub. My knee slammed into its wood base. Perfect. It was like being tangled in a giant anaconda snake, the cold copper nozzle hissing from the pressure of water left on. The ground was cold and muddy. The grass was mushy.

When I struggled to stand, someone running bumped me from behind, and I fell forward again. What was going on? People were all over the place. Boys with hooded sweatshirts and girls in white t-shirts fanned out onto the property. A bunch of them were grabbing at something. Tall trees blocked the moonlight. I dug in, alert, very Vietnam.

Voices overlapped whispering Spanish mixed with English. The Vals had crossed the deepest delta of Malibu. It looked like the entire McBride estate had been compromised. Something had to be done fast. I went into solider mode and stayed low. A small unit of girls gathered a few feet in front of me next to the shrub. Squatting made me invisible as I separated the leaves and peeked through. They were kicking something, no, someone, on the ground.

It was Rox and Claire!

I heard bells before I saw the large silver hoops. Tinkerbell and her tribe had Claire and Rox pinned, holding them by their hair. Tinkerbell yanked Claire to her feet and pulled out a giant pair of scissors from her back pocket. Poor Claire started to cry as Tinkerbell cut up Jacko the monkey: paw, tail, and then head. Claire was going to get a crew cut next. I had to do something.

"Tinkerbell!" I screamed.

The hose had me. Instead of rushing them, grabbing the scissors, and making sure Claire and Rox got away safely, I fell on my face. Tinkerbell laughed and turned away. That made me so mad I took my clog and threw it at her. The thick wooden shoe slammed into the back of her frizzy head. I heard it crack.

Again I yelled, "Tinkerbell!"

She let go of Claire and charged me like a buffalo or a rogue elephant.

"Who you calling Tinkerbell?" she barked in my face. "I'm Maldita," she stood closer, holding the top of her head. "You know what that means? It means 'cursed.' Now say it," she commanded.

"Cursed," I said, pointing my finger into her face so she knew I was cooperating. Sparks of blue shimmered from my fingertips as I watched the trails from my hand streak into the sky like a rainbow of light.

"Hey spaz," she said, slugging me in the ball of my shoulder socket. "Say my name."

No one had ever hit me so hard in my life.

"Cursed," I said.

She hit me again. Raw and full-on. Colors splashed out of her fist, and the gang of girls cheered as Tinkerbell held the scissors up in my face. She spread them wide so the blades made the shape of a V. Her thumb held them open.

"Wait a minute," I said, trying to catch my breath. That's all I could spit out before Tinkerbell grabbed a thick handful of hair hanging across my forehead and swiped the sharp blade down. Her gang laughed as she threw my hair up into the air like confetti.

That's when I snapped.

Something sounded like a mosquito buzzing loudly in my ears. I got a metal taste in my mouth. My knees buckled. Tinkerbell cut my hair. That was the end. It was the end of every rule, law, and regulation. It was the end of keeping it together. It was the end of the sweet girl. I began to burn. Everything I had been holding back about my dad, Hawaii, Jean, Uncle Mike, and trying to get everyone at State Beach to like me, exploded. I hated Tinkerbell so much it felt like the skin on my face was peeling off and fangs were growing out of my mouth. My fingers turned into claws. Black smoke poured from my ears. I was Pele.

Tinkerbell turned to her cocaptain and said something in Spanish, obviously dismissing me as some kind of loser chump. I stepped back, kicking the upside of my heel into the base of her spine. I leaned down into her face and spit out, "Tinkerbell."

Her gang thought I would start crying like Claire. They expected me to fall apart, but instead I kicked her again so Claire could make a run for it.

"We don't fight!" Rox shouted.

Part of me wanted to be a warrior and slam-dunk Tinkerbell. But I couldn't because Rox gave me another order, "Haul!" she said, running down the driveway.

I turned, not seeing that the hose had untwisted all around me. It was like getting stuck in a bunch of hula-hoops or quicksand. The more I moved or struggled, the worse it got. Tinkerbell slowly walked toward me. Her girls' smiles were getting bigger the closer they got. I might not be allowed to fight. But I could use my Hawaiian know-how and nail Tinkerbell another way. For good and for sure. I picked up the muddy nozzle of the hose, turned it to the right, and let Tinkerbell have it. A thick spray jetted right up her nose. This wasn't a gentle sprinkle. It was fire hose strong. It was so powerful, I could hold off the whole group, soak them, and sing a little song as I got up.

"Ding dong, the witch is dead, wicked witch, Valley bitch." Tinkerbell and her group didn't melt, but they sure got wet. An engine started. Nigel's van moved up toward me. Rox was yelling,

"Come on, Nani." There were streams of blue bouncing off my feet as I ran. I felt superhuman powerful. The van's headlights flashed on and off, signaling me as Nigel honked his horn.

"Nani," he insisted, revving the gas louder and faster. "Hurry." There was water everywhere. I jumped into the back of the van. As we drove away, I could see Tinkerbell's black bra shine through her t-shirt, which clung to her chest as she stood in a puddle of her own red lipstick.

CHAPTER TWENTY-SIX

Full-On

Rox had dark circles under her eyes, and she was gasping for air like a deep-sea diver with the bends. Her leather sandals were torn and wet. There were also grass stains on her velvet shorts and dirt under her fingernails.

Nigel was buckled over the steering wheel, slapping frantically to get the van in gear. The stick shift dropped down, and we lunged forward into drive. He was so crazed, he accidently turned on the windshield wipers before his headlights. Nigel's engine idled loudly. Finally he made a sharp right off the curb and onto PCH.

Rox pulled long strands of hair away from my mouth. They were no longer attached to my head.

"Oh no," I said. There was no way this could actually be happening I told myself. Nigel was driving the exact speed limit down PCH. I sat up to see a smattering of locals quickly getting into their cars and making U-turns or any turn to get them off the highway and away from the McBride estate as a row of red lights came flashing toward us. Rox looked fragile, glassy, and broken.

"Just be cool," Nigel said. The police sped past us and started turning one after another into the McBride estate. They did not circle back or attempt to pull us over.

"Okay so we aren't getting busted. Now what?" I wondered aloud.

"Everybody's meeting up at the Sunspot," Nigel said. He pushed in a John Mayall tape, and we drove silently for a while.

The Santa Ana winds were blowing hard. They made the van sway back and forth. We were just about to turn into the Sunspot. I heard metal chimes clanging, and the jukebox inside the bar was playing. It was so late, PCH was deserted except for one black-and-white cop car with its lights off, waiting for the first drunk surfer to leave the bar.

"So much for the Sunspot," Rox said.

"We're going to the bluffs." Nigel sounded strong and together but at the same time fumbled around the dash and console looking for something. At the bottom of Chautauqua Boulevard, we got a red light. Nigel dug around in the dirty ashtray.

"Found it," he said. He pushed the lighter in and held up a tiny roach between his fingertips. "Want some?" he asked. Rox and I both shook our heads and said no thank you. Nigel looked at me in the rearview mirror and winked as he took one long, giant hit.

Rox and I both knew Nigel shouldn't be lit up. Rox frowned, eyed PCH, then leaned into the front seat. She tapped Nigel's shoulder and said ever so sweetly, "We have to get Nani home in one piece."

"Totally." Nigel sat up sharply. Before he realized he had the parking brake on, the van gears grinded then jerked forward. Rox shook her head again.

"He's too stoned to drive," she said. "Nige, let's go to the bluffs and figure stuff out." Rox got a big smile on her face. Mission accomplished, until Nigel started swerving around Channel Road. After everything that had happened, it was driving with Nigel stoned that made Rox crumble. She clenched my hand. Whenever Nigel made a turn, she sucked air like it was her last breath. I remembered Mary Jo told me that both Rox's parents died in a car crash. No wonder she was so wigged. Nigel slammed on the brakes. We both fell forward. Rox had her fist in her mouth so she wouldn't scream.

"I do that sometimes," I said, pointing to Rox's fist in her mouth. Rox's eyes were shut. I don't think she heard me.

"I've got to take a wicked piss," Nigel said, skipping away and hopping behind a tree. Rox and I crawled out of the back of the van and sat on the splintered fence propped up by broken surfboards.

The bluffs were an active landslide area with a two-hundred-foot slope. The hillside was covered in thick clusters of poisonous plants with red berries and fernlike white flowers. People had tossed houseplants into the ravine with macramé string still hanging from their pots; abandoned cats roamed through the dill weed. Below all that was PCH and State Beach.

"What stinks?" I asked.

Rox pointed at the ocean. "It's red tide," she told me, lighting up a smoke and moving in to stay warm and cozy.

"Did Mary Jo give you one beer or two?" she asked.

What did that have to do with The Valleys cutting off my hair? But I knew better than to ask. I held up one finger. Rox shook her head.

"Lord Ricky told me her peace offering was spiked with Blue Cheer."

What was that? Rox read my face. I didn't want to look stupid, but she knocked on my head anyway.

"Hello? LSD—acid?"

I was almost relieved. I'd been tripping.

"Have you been seeing colors and stuff?"

I nodded.

Rox laughed, but it wasn't funny.

"Wait till you see what I do to Mary Jo." She patted my knee. "I'm gonna get her back big time."

On the bluffs it felt like time had cracked open. Like the morning my father died. Acid made my thinking super clear, and I knew there was no time to waste. This was my last chance. I needed to know if I was in the lineup, full-on. I'd never get Rox alone like this again.

I asked, "Do you like me yet?"

Rox stared out at the ocean and the moonlight. She looked like a bug. Her hair was wispy, and her big blue eyes glowed.

"I've known since I saw you. Remember that first Sunday at State?"

Of course I did. She had spotted me in the crowd and drilled her gaze right through me like the wicked Scorpion she is.

"I knew then. I knew you would . . ."

Nigel jumped right beside us, zipping up his fly.

Knew what? I wanted to say. But before I could, Nigel said, "Close your eyes, Nani."

Because I was his girlfriend, I did as I was told. Something fell over my shoulders. It was my jacket. I stumbled a bit, fumbling through the pockets searching for my rabbit foot with my eyes shut.

"Open," he said.

My blue rabbit foot was dangling off his finger around my face. He lifted it just out of reach. I jumped, trying to snag it, swinging my arms over my head.

"What'll you give me for it?"

I grabbed his face and pulled it into mine, planting a big one on his lips then wiggling my tongue all around inside his mouth, checking for wires, making sure he was the righteous babe twin.

"Do you know what you will say to your mom, Nani?" he asked.

"Sorry I screwed up tonight."

What a genius plan. I was going to tell the truth.

"And then I'll apologize," Nigel said, squeezing my hand. I turned and pointed at him.

I couldn't believe it. Nigel McBride was going to take the fall for me. He was actually going to take responsibility for my screw up. That was the most radical thing I'd ever heard. Jean would never go off on a McBride.

All the color dropped out of Rox's face as Nigel got back in the van.

I said, "Just to be on the safe side, Nigel, let's leave your van here in case my mom loses her mind for some reason." I knew that would never happen, but I couldn't stand the thought of Rox chewing her hand off just to get to my house.

All the lights in my house were on when we walked up. Crickets were sounding off all around us, and the ocean stilled smelled funky. Dogs barked, but my street was empty and pitch black.

"Are you coming with us?" I asked Rox.

"No. I'll wait," she said, shoving me forward to follow Nigel, who was taking two stairs at a time. I had to run to catch up with him. We snuck in the back door.

"Mom, I'm home."

We waited but there was no answer. The TV was blasting a John Wayne movie. I recognized his voice and cowboy talk before a round of gunfire with horses neighing sounded out.

"Maybe she's asleep?" I said.

Nigel winced. He looked really stressed with his hands clasped tight behind his back and jaw clenching out a little smile. We tiptoed down to Jean's room and peeked around her open door. The bed hadn't been slept in, and the clicker was on the carpet. John Wayne fired his gun again. *Oh no,* I thought. *What if Jean is passed out in the bathroom?* I couldn't let Nigel see that. I carefully pushed open the bathroom door.

"Mom?"

She wasn't there. We checked the patio and the living room but still no Jean. Maybe she left because of the slap, or maybe something terrible happened to her. What if she was kidnapped or dead?

Nigel whistled for Rox, who came running through the back door. "What's wrong?" Rox asked, "Where's your mom?"

"I don't know," I said.

Rox frowned and looked around.

"Wow. Your kitchen is a disaster like mine." She started munching on some grapes. I tried not to drop my jaw, but it was the first time I'd ever seen her eat, chew, and swallow. She looked around the kitchen and headed over toward a gingerbread Bundt cake Jean left by some bran muffins.

"Can I have some?" Rox asked, pointing to the cake.

I nodded, still in shock as she began eating.

"Did you and Jerry break up again?" Nigel asked her.

Rox rolled her eyes and kept chewing. With her mouth overflowing with cake, she looked like a rabid animal that didn't know the rules about eating in front of guys. It seemed that Rox had the habit of eating after a break up.

"Milk?" I asked, pointing to the fridge.

That's when I saw one of Jean's famous notes under a magnet. Each word was written boldly in a different color. It read, I TOOK THE SEVEN TO SEVEN SHIFT FOR ONE OF THE GIRLS. She had drawn angry faces in the sevens by making an upside down "u" under the number and two dots on either side. CALL! I'M AT ST. JOHN'S. —MOM

Nigel extended his arms with hands turned up. His eyes closed as he gave thanks to the Lord; then he dropped his head and said a few silent words to himself.

He asked, "Rox, you want a ride home?"

She swallowed before answering. "No, thanks," she said. "I'm spending the night here."

CHAPTER TWENTY-SEVEN

※

Taller, Thinner, and Lighter

Rox walked Nigel to the street. While they were outside, I ran
to my room and ripped apart the makeshift tent. I slammed
Mrs. Beasley under some pillows on my bed and tossed the
half-eaten Pop-Tarts in the trash. Relieved that I had gotten
it somewhat together, I raced back into the kitchen, grabbed
the ham out of the fridge, and ate it quickly. Wow, wait until
the lineup hears Rox spent the night at my house.

When she finally came back inside, it looked like I had
been chilling there the whole time. The ham and pineapple
melted in my mouth. I closed my eyes and tried to savor
every bite. I licked my sticky fingers clean. The sweet flavor
made me think of Hawaii. I was finally able to eat without breaking a rule, but now I wasn't hungry. Rox finished
chewing and talked nonstop about breaking up with Jerry
and how this time it was going to be different. This time it
was for good.

I listened patiently and waited for another chance to ask
what she knew the first time she saw me at State. Rox stared
at me, studying how I kept my lips together when I chewed

and swallowed. Every so often, I'd see some blue liquid drip from her hair, but I knew better than to mention it. If she knew I was still tripping, she'd never tell me about her first impression of me or how I ranked with the lineup.

Something was buzzing in my face. I ignored it. I wasn't sure it was really there or not until Rox clapped her hands next to my ear and smashed a fly dead on the counter. When I jumped back, she lectured me about never swimming when there was a red tide. There were too many bugs and too much kelp in the ocean. Then out of nowhere she said, "Let's take a shower."

Rox was totally wet by the time I got the nerve to follow her to the bathroom. I had no choice but to get naked. It was like I was taking a shower with one of my centerfolds, and the reality was almost too much. I swung the curtains aside and made a complete turn as I entered the shower. I didn't look at Rox and did my best to shield the front of my body from her. I was surprisingly cool until I slipped on the oily tiles and nearly fell face first. It was like dropping into a wave too late and losing my balance before hitting the curl. I always laughed when a guy did that, but it wasn't so funny when it was me making a fool of myself. Rox looked smaller with her hair slicked back. She grabbed my hand.

"Whoa, the boat's still rocking," I said.

"No, it's the shea butter," Rox told me. "I use it to keep my skin from peeling. Hold onto me," she said as she placed my hands above the curve of her waist. My arms locked around her as she pulled me in. I loved the way she was so bossy.

Our bodies pressed together, my chest to her back. I nestled between her shoulder blades and spit out hot water as it rolled off her head and into my mouth. Maybe I was relieved knowing I was on acid and not going crazy. Or maybe it was Rox or maybe it was the steam that surrounded us, but for the first time in ages I felt good.

Rox reached her arms up and held her bathing suit under the nozzle. She used her fingernails to dig out sand from each tiny seam. She scooped up my hair from around my lower back and poured Herbal Essence onto the tips, lathering from the bottom, up, until she reached my scalp to scrub away the loose hairs.

"How bad is it?" I asked.

"Not bad." She repeated the processes of gathering and lathering. "Your voice sounds sexy like that, all hoarse."

After we were dry, we sat in the bathroom and Q-tipped the sand out of our ears. Rox went through Jean's drawers until she found what she was looking for. She sat me down on the bathroom counter and said, "Don't move."

Rox stood over me on her tippy-toes. "This won't hurt, I promise," she combed out the jagged parts of my hair, and then, using Jean's tiny cuticle scissors, began to even out the entire mess, trimming small sections at a time. When I was finally given permission to look in the mirror, I was blown away by what she had done. I had ultra-short, half-inch bangs across my forehead. Rox blended the rest of my hair into layers like fish scales, one overlapping the other. It made me look taller, thinner, and lighter. It was a new look to go with the whole new me. No one on the mainland or Hawaii had long hair like mine now. It made me look boss, one of a kind, totally glam surf, and better than before.

CHAPTER TWENTY-EIGHT

※

Fiji

We walked into my room. Rox turned on the red lava lamp. She picked up my favorite elephant necklace with one hand and the picture of Dad and me with the other.

"Do you miss him?" she asked.

"Yeah, I do. He gave me that necklace on my last birth-day." That was the most I had talked about my dad to Rox.

Rox waited for me to say more, but I didn't. I wouldn't. She told me she didn't miss her dad at all. I found that hard to believe, but then Rox told me the whole story. She said, "My dad used to practice CPR on me. He gave me regular 'check-ups' when I started getting boobs."

"Why?" I asked.

Rox ignored my question and continued. "CPR hurts," she said, poking the middle of my chest, then my arms, try-ing to get me to laugh.

Maybe if I knew CPR, I could have saved my dad. I had never thought that before. What if he didn't have to die? What if it was my fault?

Rox put two fingers on my wrist and then on my neck.

"No pulse," she said. "Lie down."

I lay flat on my back. She pinched my nose and put her lips to mine. I tried to pull away, but she shoved me down.

"Do you want to learn CPR or not?"

When I lay down again, she blew into my mouth. My cheeks filled with air and bloated out like a pufferfish. Rox pretended to check my pulse again, but I was laughing so hard I couldn't lie still.

"Look," she said. "Do you want to save lives or not?"

I nodded, yes. I really did want to.

This time, Rox didn't pinch my nose at all. She rested her lips on top of mine and pressed them down into what felt like a kiss. She lifted my chin and tilted my head back, pushed her lips against mine, and then rested her head on my chest.

"Now, you practice on me."

I had forgotten where to start, but Rox patiently showed me step by step. Then she lay down and held her breath. I mean, really stopped breathing.

Not even those pearl divers in Japan could hold their breath as long as Rox. I was pushing on her chest like she showed me, counting to fifteen and everything. But she wouldn't breathe. Her face went from pink to kind of purplish blue and when her lips started to change colors, I got worried. I said her name over and over, but she didn't move.

I tilted her head back, lifted her chin, and opened her mouth. Then I pressed my lips hard onto hers. I was just about to pinch her nose and blow into her mouth when she wrapped her arms around my shoulders and pulled me in close.

"Claire taught me how to hold my breath." Then she smiled and pushed her tongue into my mouth and we kissed. I accidentally touched the side of her breast but pulled away fast. I did not want her to think I was weird.

"How'd you learn to kiss like that?" Rox asked.

"Marshmallows," I answered.

Rox looked puzzled and amused at the same time.

The records on my turntable were stacked starting with Joni Mitchell's *Ladies of the Canyon*. When Rox flipped the switch, she listened and said, "I love Joni," like she was her best friend or something.

It was the first time I had ever seen Rox without her waterproof mascara. She looked younger. Also, wearing my flannel nightgown and slippers, she looked downright sweet.

"Would you like to go to Fiji with me?" she asked, tickling the inside of my hand.

I rolled onto my side and thought before I answered. I imagined us running away together. Maybe we could find an apartment, work as stewardesses, and get fake IDs. It would be great to go to Fiji with Rox. We could kiss all the time, get a cat, name it Jerry, and be best friends forever.

"Yeah, definitely," I told her.

Rox turned off the lava lamp next to my bed. Her silhouette moved closer, and her teeth glowed white in the dark. I hoped we were going to practice-kiss some more, but she tugged at my robe and said, "Let's cuddle."

Rox nuzzled against my ear and nestled her body into me real close.

"I love to cuddle," she said, twisting the nightgown around her thigh. I waited for her to continue, but she didn't. She just wrapped her arms around my midsection and pressed her nose into my neck. I guessed we were going to sleep. Lying all tucked in was the best feeling I ever had.

I tried to breathe at the same time Rox did. It was like Double Dutch jump rope, trying to step in at the right time. Matching Rox's rhythm was nearly impossible with my heart beating fast until she softly hummed off key with Joni Mitchell's song "The Circle Game." Then I relaxed into her.

Rox etched her name into my arm with her fingertips.

"Are we going to play the tickle game?" I asked.

The tickle game felt so good. I closed my eyes and let Rox swirl the tip of her finger slowly up the inside of my arm. When she got to the middle part, just on the other side of my elbow, I was supposed to stop her. That was the point of the game. But I let her keep going all the way to my shoulder because I didn't want her to ever stop. She said, "I'm too hot in this."

She took off the nightgown. Naked on her side in the dark, she looked better than Miss December. She was flawless. The curve of her waist was just an inch from my hand. If I moved even a tiny bit I could touch her. But that inch might as well have been a million miles.

"You wanna go to Fiji?" Rox asked again.

I thought to myself, *How great would that be—living on an island, in the middle of nowhere, with Rox?* "I'm packed and ready." I tried to look casual without moving any closer to her and kept an eye on that inch between us.

She smiled so I smiled. She pulled at the tie of my robe.

"It's hot in Fiji. You better take this off," she said.

I didn't want to look like a prude, so I did what she said and laid back down. The distance between us didn't last long. Rox rolled over me to the other side of the bed.

"Now, pretend you're Jerry."

We clutched each other tightly. It was like we were one person, hair tangled, bodies glued together until the third Joni Mitchell record flopped down and was halfway over. She pushed and squeezed herself tightly before letting go of the grip she had around my shoulders.

"Now, pretend I'm Nigel," she told me.

When we were done, I was on the other side of reality.

☀

Rox and I sat at the kitchen table eating Koo Koo Supremes. We pulled the candy apart, letting the marshmallow and caramel fall into our hands. Then we chewed the pecans one at a time. When we were stuffed, we smoked my last Lark 100, which I had hidden away for a special occasion.

"Was that your first trip to Fiji?" Rox asked.

"Yeah," I said, pulling some chewy cream from between her fingers. "Did you ever go to Fiji with Claire?" I asked.

Rox belted out a giant, very un-Rox-like laugh. It looked like candy was going to squirt out her nose. She gave me a little kick and said, "Claire doesn't even know Fiji exists. It's too far away for her."

"So I was the first expedition?" I asked.

"No," Rox said. Then she took my hand and assured me, "But you were the best trip ever."

I wanted to kiss Rox but knew a smile would do. After all, we weren't in Fiji any more.

It was 4:00 a.m. Most of the colors had stopped swirling around, but I still felt speedy and wired. The ground did not feel firm under my feet so I held onto the walls as I walked back to my room with Rox. We took aspirin and brushed our teeth before we got back into bed.

Rox lay next to me and touched my hand. I think she thought I was asleep already, but I wasn't. She turned off the record player and turned the lava lamp back on.

She said, "I hate the dark." And then she turned to me. "You probably won't remember this, but I'm going to watch over you now."

I kept my eyes shut and listened as Rox settled herself next to me. She kissed me on the cheek, turned onto her side, and flipped her hair over my pillow. Then she pushed her butt next to mine and pulled my feet around hers. It was quiet for a moment.

"I know you're awake," she said.

That made me smile. I could have twisted back into her arms, snuggled that not-so-tan spot under her chin, and started another trip to Fiji, but instead I lay still and listened to her hum a little tune. It sounded like a Beach Boys song. I'm not sure which one. Her voice was even more off-key than before. Then she started counting backward softly from one hundred. My heart felt too big for my chest as I closed my eyes and silently counted along.

CHAPTER TWENTY-NINE

Happy Face

I woke up still butt to butt with Rox. I pressed my body against hers. It felt good to have her next to me. We were friends; finally it was real. Something great had happened. Actually, it was beyond great. All the stars and planets were aligned; nothing was in retrograde or eclipsed by uncertainty anymore. I wanted to kiss Rox good morning, but instead I said, "I love you."

"I love you, too," Jean said.

My eyes sprung open. I went bananas when Jean rolled over with smelly wino breath and put her arms around me. I covered my head with a pillow and froze.

"Let's not fight anymore," she said.

Where had Rox gone? The flannel nightgown was folded neatly on the chair, my albums were stacked and put away. I noticed that my entire room was clean. That was weird.

I gave Jean the *shaka* sign. I spread my pinky and thumb wide then twisted my wrist side to side like locals in Hawaii do. But inside I was dying.

Jean said, "Let's be honest with each other, okay?"

"Okay," I said. "You drink too much."

She immediately pushed herself away and stomped out of my room, slamming the door behind her. Within seconds, she pushed it open again and tossed a letter at me like it was a Frisbee. Then asked, "Are those bangs?"

I shoved the pillow tighter over my face and yelled, "Go away!"

"Why didn't you just shave your whole head? And clean your sheets. There's sand everywhere."

Jean slammed the door and marched down the hall.

I pulled the covers over my head and curled into a little ball, wondering how so much sand got in my bed. I felt around under my pillow and realized it wasn't sand; it was my dad!

Mrs. Beasley had split open. The seam of her belly was torn just enough for a clump of powdery ash to spill onto the sheets. I jumped out of bed and quickly got two album covers to scoop him up with. Then I emptied his pot stash out of the glass pickle jar into a shoebox and poured his loose ashes from Mrs. Beasley's belly into it. I screwed the lid on tight and put him next to my bed. My cuticles were outlined in white powder.

That's when it dawned on me like a big strobe light going off in my face. I was turning into Jean. My dad was next to my bed. Not in a pretty box but in an old jar. It was time. I had to let him go or else I'd be no better than her.

I looked down at the tips of my hair. It was like they had been coated in dry cement. My father's ashes were firmly embedded in the wet strands. I grabbed a fistful of hair and tried to shake him out, flailing my head side to side. I panicked. It made me feel as if I had fallen into a spider nest and thousands of baby spiders were crawling on my head and face. I ran to the bathroom, turned on the hot water, and soaked the bottom of my hair in the sink until it steamed so much I could barely see myself in the mirror. My weird eyes seemed greener. How could that be? Maybe it was from the acid or from messing around with a guy and a girl in one night. Something about me was not the same.

The room spun a little, and my forehead felt like someone slammed a board across it. But there were no sparks, and nothing was dancing off my walls. I sprayed some disinfectant on my hair and twisted it up into a knot, sticking a pencil through it to make a bun. Then I picked up the letter Jean had tossed. Finally, something from Annie. I cracked open the shutters for some light and read.

Dear Haunani,

Better you be with some banana buddahead squid than a keke face haole like Nigel McBride. Whssamatta you? Goin mainland? Nevah suck face with shahkbait. Don't care how cute or rich he is. White skin is for white skin. Finda poi dog hapa like yourself.

Annie made Lord Ricky and Claire look like lightweight racists from the way she trashed people. She went off on

Japanese, whites, and everyone between like me. What was her problem? I didn't understand until I finished reading:

> Howzit with Jerry? Get rid of his double-eyed girl, the one who wears mascara to the beach. And tell your moddah she's snapped selling that brahla Mike Kei the Jones. Your moddah waha is maxed out and you will be too if you don't go back to smoking Kools and acting mo' bettah. Eh Haunani?
>
> Don't ever come home with a haole like McBride or I will kick your ass.
>
> ~~Love~~, Annie

Annie had gotten all *tita* on me. I should have never written about my new friends to her, but I thought she'd be stoked. True, Mike Kei was a good-for-nothing jerk. But she had no right to trash my friends or call my mom a *haole* bitch. As if using pidgin would code her warnings.

That's when I wrote my first official rule:

**Never go off on somebody's mother unless
it's your own.**

This rule went beyond "the rules." Annie no longer had both oars in the water, if she ever did. She liked pointing the finger at everyone but herself. It seemed for Annie writing rules was easier than following them. As if I would snag Jerry, dump Nigel, and stab my Rox in the back because she told me to. I turned her letter over and wrote: New Rule #2:

Treat people the way you want to be treated.

Jean banged stuff around the kitchen then everything went quiet until my alarm clock went off. It startled me. KHJ was blasting the morning Top Ten. It was 9:00 a.m.

"Honey, would you come into the kitchen now?"

It was time for the big punishment. I was going to have to come up with some answers as to why I didn't call, why I was late, why this, and why that. I tied my robe tight, pulled the sleeves down as far as they would go, and lifted the collar high around my neck. Then I shuffled down the hallway, saying a little prayer. *Please Jesus, if you get me out of this one, I promise to do something seriously Christian. Just please, get me out of this one. Amen.*

The kitchen was abnormally clean, too. All the counters had been cleared; the dishes were washed and put away. The pots and pans were washed. There were even flowers in a vase on the table. When I opened the refrigerator to avoid eye contact with Jean, not only was it clean, but everything inside was totally organized. All the sauces, like Tabasco and Worcester, were lined up next to one another, and an open can of corn had foil wrapped tightly around its top. Even the cabinets had been set up so the big bags of flour were in the back and little boxes of raisins, cereal, and bouillon cubes were up front.

"Sit down," Jean instructed me.

Here it comes, I thought.

Jean was still in her nursing uniform. She was looking at me, doing the silent stare thing.

I rested my chin on the inside of my hand and stared back at her.

"Thank you for cleaning the house," she said.

I shrugged my shoulders and acted like I knew what she was talking about. It was a total *Twilight Zone*. The whole house shined, and I mean everywhere; even the living room ashtrays were empty. If Jean didn't do it, and I didn't do it, who did?

We sat in silence. Jean took a dramatic breath in and out. No doubt Jean would try and ground me for life. Or take something away, but what? Most likely, it would be the shopping spree she promised when the big bucks from the Java Jones came in. I guess going to Judy's and Vin Baker's for shoes were treats I could kiss goodbye. There's probably no way I'd get the big birthday bash at Trader Vic's after this bust either.

I watched her light a cigarette and hoped she'd blow some smoke my way. She had a serious look on her face.

Finally she said, "Mrs. McBride called me early this morning at St. John's. I know the whole story."

I dropped my throbbing forehead on the table. I was up a creek without a paddle. There was nothing to say so I waited.

"Mrs. McBride explained that supper was late because her fundraiser in Santa Barbara ran over and she told me all about the unfortunate incident with that drug-crazed girl from the valley. Are you all right?" Jean looked concerned.

I looked up with just my eyes. What was going on?

Jean wrapped her fingers around my bruised forearm. She took my scrunched-up face as a signal to start acting all motherly. She put her hand on mine. I looked at her white skin on my tan and thought about how weird it must have been for her to live in Hawaii all those years, so very pink, and so very disliked. I put my other hand on hers.

"I was so worried," she said, "until Agnes explained everything to me."

Why wasn't I in trouble? Then, talk about being saved by the bell, the phone rang.

"Maybe it's Uncle Mike," I said.

"That'll be the day." Jean put out her cigarette.

I wanted a smoke so badly. Maybe once I figured out what was going on, I'd treat myself to a powdered donut and a carton of Larks, not those lame-ass, mentholated Kools Annie toked on.

"Hello?" Jean said.

She got a big smirk on her face and turned her back toward me for privacy. Maybe she had a boyfriend?

"So nice of you to call," Jean continued.

It sounded like she was talking to Nixon or some other person she thought was important. She stood upright with her shoulders back. Her voice was smooth and soft. She took long, slow drags from a newly lit cigarette as she listened, agreeing every so often.

"Thank you, Agnes," she said.

Agnes who? Jean waved me to the phone, impatiently.

She covered the receiver with her hand and mouthed, "It's Mrs. McBride."

She handed the phone to me.

No way was I ever talking to Mrs. McBride again. I shook my head and backed off, but Jean insisted. She almost shoved the phone down my throat. I had to take it.

"Hello?"

"Did you miss me?"

It was Rox.

"Yes, Mrs. McBride, I did."

Jean was impressed with my manners. I tried not to smile too much as Rox relayed her conversations with my mother back to me. Rox had apologized to Jean, as Mrs. McBride, for all the stuff about me missing my curfew, and she told her about the awful girl who had invaded her home in Malibu last night. Rox sounded just like her.

Then in her own voice she said, "Meet me at Roy's in twenty minutes."

"Thank you, Mrs. McBride. I will."

I hung up the phone. Jean said, "She's a very nice woman, you know."

I felt bad lying to Jean, but it wasn't like she was going to run into the real Mrs. McBride anytime soon.

"Yes, Mom, I know," I said. I followed her down the dark hall, watching her shuffling in ballet slippers half on and half off, a bottle of beer in her hand. She stepped out of her uniform. I saw a roll of skin hanging over her half-slip, her bra was on its last hooks and red imprints from her uniform being too tight crisscrossed along her back. Jean's skin wiggled like an old lady's. Her tan lines were gone, and her hair had lost its flip. She had no aloha left. Poor Jean had wilted into an Eleanor Rigby right before my very eyes. Now she was just a sad Beatles song.

"Be back from the beach at five-ish. I'm cooking cod."

Jean didn't even know I was looking at her. She closed the door.

CHAPTER THIRTY

Bowie Bangs

Rox and Claire stood in front of Canyon Beach Wear next to Roy's, pretending to look at the bright-colored suits in the window. From their posture, arms crossed and heads almost touching, I could see they were having a serious discussion as Rox waved me over.

Rox had dark circles under her eyes but still looked outstanding in her white, bell-sleeved muslin blouse and silver conch belt hanging low on her hips. The blouse was open, of course, to show off a new bikini. I was surprised to see my elephant necklace from Dad nestled around her neck. It hung above her cleavage like it had always been there. I wasn't sure if I was stoked or upset.

Claire stood next to Rox, looking like a lemon verbena cookie, just like she did the first day I laid eyes on her, hair perfectly parted down the middle, turquoise dangling earrings, and today she wore a backless, cotton micro mini dress with white flip-flops. There was no hug hello. They were all business. Something was going on. The clothes, the conference, the whispering. I was afraid Claire knew I kissed Shawn. Or even worse, maybe Rox told Claire about Fiji.

Claire inspected my ultra-low shorts, crocheted bathing suit top, and tied-up silk shirt. I couldn't look her in the eyes, so I put my shades on. I felt so bad about Shawn. What would I say if she brought it up?

"I see what you mean," Claire said, touching my one-inch bangs and smiling. Then she turned to Rox and said, "Very Bowie."

I had seen a picture of David Bowie in *CREEM* magazine. He was amazing. I was going to get his new album *Ziggy Stardust and the Spiders from Mars.* I wished I was on Mars right then when Claire and Rox started whispering, hands in front of their mouths. Especially when Rox said, "Claire."

"Yes, Rox?"

"I have to pee. Will you keep watch?"

"Sure."

It was like they were reciting the Pledge of Allegiance. It was so rehearsed.

"Come on, Nani." Rox gave me one of her pushes and moved me forward.

CHAPTER THIRTY-ONE

Sisters of Sand

There was no bathroom at Roy's. That meant we had to go in the gas station. Rox quickly steered me through the parking lot. Then instead of going into the Chevron, she guided me down a small pathway between the buildings. The space looked like a narrow version of Jean's garden with weeds and succulents everywhere. It was overgrown. Trudging through the plants made my legs itch.

"I thought you had to pee?"

Rox didn't answer. That wasn't a good sign.

Obviously this wasn't the right moment to ask her, but I had to know, "When did you sleep?"

"I didn't."

"How did you clean up so fast?"

"I just did. Come on. We don't have much time."

Rox nudged me forward down the alley.

The sound of power tools drilling metal got louder and louder. She stopped before we turned the corner and lifted my shades up onto my head.

"Check this out," she said. I could see three men in blue overalls covered in grease with baseball caps on backward and long ponytails stuck through them. They were like surgeons holding body parts, examining mufflers and the underneath part of a tow truck. They acknowledged Rox and went back to work. Rox identified them one at a time.

"That's See No Evil underneath the truck on that metal slippery thing. That's Hear No Evil. And that's Speak No Evil with the metal hoodie on his head." Rox was talking so fast I could barely keep up. "In mechanic's land, everyone is invisible. They let us pretty much do anything we want back here because the Topangas do the big deals out of sight. I think they give them like 10 percent of everything they grow." Speak No Evil pulled the metal welding mask over his face, lit his torch, and turned away. It was like we really were invisible.

Rox dug into the bottom of her purse and pulled me back into the shadows. She took out a needle and thread.

"I always keep this for bikini emergencies."

That was good advice. But weird considering everything was fitting her just fine at the moment. She pulled the needle out of the spool and dropped the thread back into her purse.

She held the needle between her fingers, then instructed me to hold up my hand, placing my forefinger straight out. "This might hurt a little." It looked like she was going to jab the needle into me like Norman Bates did in *Psycho*, killing Janet Leigh, quickly and with a lot of screaming.

"Whoa, whoa," I yanked my hand away and held it tightly against my chest.

Rox pointed her little needle at me. "You know what I knew the moment you walked onto State Beach? I knew you were going to be in the lineup. Someday you are going to rule and be more intense than Claire and I ever could be. You know what else I knew? I knew you were the Fiji type."

The smile that spread across my face was unstoppable. This was so far beyond anything I could have imagined.

"So that's what this is all about."

"Yeah. Now give me your hand and stop smiling. Do you have any idea how dangerous Fiji is? "

She was so intense. What was the big deal?

She grabbed my wrist and stuck my finger before I could say ouch.

"Did that hurt?"

"Yeah."

"Good, remember that because you don't have any idea what would happen to us if the word got out about Fiji. Now do it to me."

I poked the needle into Rox. A circle of blood oozed from the tip just like mine. We pushed our fingers together. One of the Evils started using a jackhammer in the garage. I could barely hear what Rox was saying. I leaned in with my ear close to her mouth.

"We could get tarred and feathered, run off of State Beach. Nobody can know about Fiji, Nani. Do you understand that once and for all?" I nodded. "Then swear you'll never tell anyone. Swear on your dead father. Swear on your eyeballs. Swear on what's left of your hair, and swear to me forever."

"I swear."

Rox kissed me on the lips and said, "Okay, let's go." She grabbed my hand and yanked me forward, skipping over the plants back into broad daylight. Claire tapped her wrist impatiently when she saw us, and Rox lifted her chin all tough. She turned back to me with a few last words of advice.

"If you ever want to see Fiji again, remember this. No matter what happens from this moment on, promise me you will never lose it. If your feelings get hurt, if you want to say something—don't. Swear again."

"I swear."

"Now we're going to take care of some official business. Welcome to the Sisters of Sand." She slid my shades back down to my face.

CHAPTER THIRTY-TWO

Adiós

Across the street, we saw the lineup file out of State Liquor with cartons of cigarettes. None of them looked hungover from the party last night. Each girl held a Tab. They were using Red Vines for straws. Something had them laughing so hard they were holding their sides.

"Making quite a spectacle out of themselves, aren't they?" Rox said to Claire and me. Claire was looking past the lineup toward PCH.

"Oh no," she said. Rox turned around.

"What's he doing here?" she asked.

I peeked over my shoulder. A police car put on his siren and flashing lights. Across the street, the lineup stopped in their tracks. Cartons of cigarettes were tossed from one girl to the next like hot potatoes until they made their way to the largest purse. The Lisas started brushing their hair while lingering at the stoplight. Mary Jo ducked behind them. KC, Jenni, and Suzie sat all innocent-like at the bus stop. They looked like sweet little teenagers getting organized for a day at the beach as they watched the police car pulling up in front of Rox, Claire, and me.

"I'll handle this," Rox said with more command than ever. She let her shirt drop off her shoulders, pushed her boobs up high and flipped her hair back over her head. In the snap of a finger, she transformed herself into a dominator.

"Hi, Officer Walzcuk," she said.

A fake smile worthy of an Academy Award was plastered on her face. The way she pulled it together was unreal. Oh my God, Rox was good.

Officer Terry Walzcuk was the local beat cop. He looked like a Libra. He had a belly and white hair that receded into two sharp points on his very high forehead. It was a perfect summer morning and almost eighty degrees, but Officer Walzcuk wasn't even sweating. He must have been uncomfortable in his dark long-sleeved uniform with the big heavy gun belt squeezed under his gut. His mirrored shades made it impossible for me to tell where he was looking or what he was looking at. What got me all tense was he had left his engine running. That couldn't be a good sign.

"Hello, Missy," Officer Walzcuk said to Rox. "Were you at the party last night?"

I didn't hear what Rox said, but I saw Claire signal the lineup. One by one, each girl put on a super-smooth smile and walked across the street. It was like seeing a canoe race where everyone's moves are synchronized. The lineup floated toward us in unison, stopping traffic. Even some gay men whistled at them; they were that beautiful.

Watching the lineup, I knew anywhere would be somewhere just because they were there. They closed in around me, and I felt it. Locals were like family, and I was finally a part of this one surrounded by sisters.

"Cute bangs," Mary Jo blurted out as she touched my head and laughed.

I wanted to slap her, but I had just sworn on my eyeballs to stay calm no matter what. I lowered my head and concentrated on Fiji. I let the Lisas dote over my bangs as Officer Walzcuk checked us out, toes to nose.

"Who got assaulted last night?" he bellowed.

Without hesitating, Mary Jo and Suzie pointed at me.

"She did," they said at once.

Officer Walzcuk took me aside.

He asked for my full name and address. He wanted to know if my parents knew I was out last night.

"My mother did," I told him.

"What about your father?" he asked.

"My dad is dead." I folded my arms across my chest and said it again. "My dad is dead." I did everything I could not to cry. I squeezed my butt tight and curled my toes, but my eyes still watered up. Even so, I wasn't about to let myself really cry. No friggin' way.

"How'd he die?" Officer Walzcuk asked.

"Heart attack," I said, looking down at the ground.

"That's too bad. Habla español, Señorita?" he asked in a super-loud voice. I turned around to see Mary Jo and Suzie laughing it up, while the other girls rolled their eyes. Officer Walzcuk took me by my shoulders and turned me to face him.

"Why are you speaking Spanish?" I asked.

"Because you're Mex-eee-caa-n," he said, exaggerating the syllables so the whole world could hear him.

"No," I said, gritting down a smile and pulling off my shades to reveal my *haole* green eyes. I wanted to sound out *I'm Ha-waii-an*, just the way he said Mexican, but I knew better. Dad told me that police officers were unpredictable. He said I should watch out for cops, especially the big white ones.

"I'm Hawaiian," I explained, shifting my body weight from one side to the other and smiling bigger. I even dipped my eyes and looked up at him just like Rox did. If she had been watching, she would have been so proud of me for that.

"Oh, like 'Book 'em Danno?'" the moron asked. He got sort of excited. He went from treating me like dirt to getting all starstruck.

I was never going to live that show down. Maybe that was okay.

"You've got it exactly," I said.

Without another word, he slipped his arm around my waist and moved me to the patrol car. If he hadn't had such a big grin on his face, I would've sworn he was going to arrest me.

"Is this the girl who attacked you?" He sounded concerned.

Tinkerbell sat in the back seat with her hands cuffed in plastic ties. In daylight, she looked ghoulish with light blue eye shadow and mascara caked under her swollen brown eyes.

"Take your time," Officer Walzcuk said.

He led me closer to the car for a better look. I gave Tinkerbell a thorough once over. Not because I needed to, I just wanted to make her sweat while I played along with Officer Moron.

"It's not her," I finally said.

"Are you sure?" he asked.

I paused. Just to give Tinkerbell one more kick in the ass, let her worry for a minute more that I'd fink on her. Let her squirm.

"Yeah, I'm positive," I said. "The girl from last night was thinner and prettier."

Then Officer Moron had the entire lineup and everyone at Roy's, including Roy and Darlene, come out of the restaurant to look at Tinkerbell.

"Her name is Angela Espiñoza," Officer Moron said, "but she goes by Maldita, 'The Cursed.'"

He grinned as he said her name, sucked in his gut with a deep breath, and tucked his thumbs into his belt loops to make a serious final statement. The guy obviously watched too much TV. Talk about a McGarrett complex.

"If anyone sees her around here again, call the police immediately."

He talked as if he were giving a press conference about Charles Manson or something. *How lame*, I thought. I looked at Rox and Claire as they chatted him up, sealing the deal. The rest of the lineup was flirting with Roy, trying to get free cups of coffee. It gave me a chance to get one last look at Tinkerbell. She didn't move, but her eyes shifted slowly up toward me.

"You're nothing but a honky wannabe," she said, then spit to one side.

Oh great. Yet another word for haole. I'd never been called a honky before. I leaned against the patrol car and spoke through the crack in the window so she wouldn't miss a word I was about to say.

"Get a good look at these green eyes, Tinkerbell." I stared at her. "They give me a right-of-way to both lanes of the highway, if you catch my drift. The best of both worlds." I turned to leave, but on second thought, I had one more thing to say. "Oh, by the way, thanks for the trim. It's really working out. Very Bowie, don't you think?" I gave her the finger and said, "That's for Jacko," and walked away.

The war between us had officially begun.

"Aloha," Officer Moron said as he opened the car door and got in.

"Bye, Officer Walzcuk," we all said with big, fake girl smiles.

The patrol car made a U-turn onto PCH. Maybe Tinkerbell would go to jail, or maybe he'd drop her back in the valley. Any which way, it wasn't my business anymore. Rox and Claire steered me toward the lineup waiting at Roy's.

"Let's get this over with," Rox said.

And with that, Claire moved into action big time.

CHAPTER THIRTY-THREE

Six Forks

Claire strolled up to the front of Roy's and spoke to the lineup slowly.

"Mary Jo, could you set up today?" she said as she slipped her arm over Suzie's shoulder. Nailing the space at the beach for the day was an honor, and I was pissed that Mary Jo, the traitor, was picked to do it. I had to look away and think about Fiji again. Mary Jo was stoked and a big smile flashed across her face. *Very uncool.*

"Sure," Mary Jo said.

"Suz, can you help her out?"

Suzie nodded. Being the next in line to rule, she knew exactly where to put everyone's towel and how to position them so they faced the sun.

"So, you want coffee?" Claire asked Mary Jo.

"Cream and two sugars."

The nerve of her. Claire just gave a cheerful double thumbs-up to Mary Jo and handed over her towel along with Rox's. The Lisas piled theirs on, too. Jenni tossed hers to Suzie. KC, the loner, had already headed over to the volleyball courts.

It was dead inside Roy's thanks to red tide and a swell that hit down south in Huntington. We had the place all to ourselves. Darlene poured us coffee. "And two to go, please," Jenni said. She passed me a cigarette. I took a long drag. Finally. A smoke.

"The regular?" Darlene asked. Rox nodded. *Thank you, Jesus,* I thought. *I get to eat.* But before I could order, Darlene gave us six forks and said, "I'll be right back with that sticky bun."

Claire swirled a spoon around in her coffee then tapped the side of the mug. There was no room for my elbows on the table. I sat up straight in the pew-like booth. Both my legs stuck to the bench planks. Claire asked, "Are we all agreed then?"

The table fell silent. The Lisas leaned forward and nodded. Rox looked at each girl. One by one they answered, "Agreed."

"Agreed on what?" Jenni asked.

I thought they were going to war with the Vals. There was no way. Tinkerbell would kick our butts.

"Can I say one thing?" I asked, raising my hand.

Everyone except Rox said yeah right away.

"Going after her isn't worth it."

The Lisas rolled their eyes.

"You're way too nice, Nani," Lisa Y. said.

"If Mary Jo had dosed me, I'd totally kill her." Lisa H. added.

Rox threw her hands up in the air and slammed her fork down on the table. Everyone went silent again. Rox lit another cigarette and spoke softly to the group.

"Claire and I have some bad news." She covered her mouth, trying to keep from being overheard. She motioned for everyone to lean in and tapped Claire to take over.

"You might've noticed that I sent Suzie with Mary Jo." Claire paused briefly and looked around to make sure all of us were listening.

"Suzie was in on it, too," she said.

"No way," Jenni blurted out.

"Way," Claire said. "Lord Ricky told me everything this morning. Mary Jo bought the acid from him, but it was Suzie who opened the front gate. It wasn't an accident those Valleys got in."

Claire watched Rox rearrange the salt and pepper, then the cream and sugar into order by size. Before she could start cleaning the table, Claire gently put her hand over Rox's and continued.

"And this, everybody has to swear to never tell," she whispered. "Rox got dosed, too. She hasn't slept in over twenty-four hours, thanks to chugging Nani's beer. She's been on a cleaning binge."

Rox kept bouncing her leg up and down. She lifted her coffee cup and wiped the table beneath it clean. Then she wiped the windowsill behind her, flicking a dead fly to the next table. Everyone was watching but knew better than to say anything.

"You know acid is like speed," Lisa Y. said in her raspy voice.

Jenni looked like she was going to cry and Claire started to fume. They used each other's cigarettes to light up, waited until Darlene served the food, and then shook their heads in disbelief.

Lisa H. said, "Then Suzie's out, too."

No one said a word. Forks were suspended in mid-air and cigarettes dangled from fingers. Claire stepped up the conversation, "Suzie wanted to get back at Nani."

"Why?" I asked. I had been nothing but nice to Suzie.

Rox looked at me like, "Hello," then pointed to the medal around my neck.

Claire knocked on my head as if it were wood.

"Anyone in there?" she laughed.

"Nigel?" I asked.

"You aced him," said Lisa H.

"Totally," Lisa Y. smiled.

Jenni hiccupped loudly, looking out the window. "Um, can we get back to some facts?" she asked and hiccupped again.

"No. It could've been any one of us who drank the wrong beer. Christ, Jenni, it could have been you," Rox said.

"Yeah, what if you ended up on a table, half-naked, doing the hula in front of every surfer on the west coast?" Lisa H. asked.

Everyone agreed. Under the table, Rox put her hand on top of my knee and squeezed. I sat up and smiled, too.

"At least Nani looked hot doing it," Rox said. She flipped her hair back like a whip, put a dollar on the table, and strut out of Roy's.

"I'm sorry, Jen," Claire said, sidestepping out of the booth. The lineup followed behind her, gingerly ushering Jenni out onto the street. "We can't trust either of them now."

I stood up quickly. A whooshing sound in my ears made me sway back and forth. The cash register popped open and clanged as I snuck the last bite of sticky bun and hurried after the lineup.

CHAPTER THIRTY-FOUR

Killer

I charged down the stairs with the lineup into the tunnel below PCH. Each girl glanced at the others, fully understanding what was going to happen next. They had done this walk so many times it was routine. But for me it was mind-boggling. Rox lit up.

"It takes away the stink," she said, handing me a smoke.

"Cigarettes are great weapons," Lisa Y. said. She jabbed her Virginia Slim at the air, fighting off imaginary demons.

"Seriously," Rox said, "always stay lit in the underpass."

How simple was that? She was just so smart. I looked at Rox, hoping to catch her eye, but it was too dark and we were hauling. As a group, we moved with a speed that made men fall to either side of the dim passageway. Their outlines smelled of cologne and tanning oils. But we girls were like windswept UFOs thrusting ourselves out the chute and into the light.

Lord Ricky greeted us in his English accent.

"Good morning, ladies," he said, taking off his visor. "How are we feeling today?" he asked, looking directly at me.

I guess my face showed how I felt, because Rox shook her head at me and frowned. I wanted to punch him, but I told myself not to go there and remembered the Fiji oath. But someday I'd get him back.

The volleyball courts were crowded; two games were going on. The old guys were greased and soaking up the rays with reflectors under their chins. The rest of the beach was another story. I had never seen it so empty.

"It's the red tide," Rox said.

That's what smelled so fishy.

"Stinks, doesn't it?" Rox asked.

I swear she could read my mind like we were linked or something. She smiled and winked.

"This is gonna work out just fine," she said, taking Claire's arm in hers.

It didn't bother me at all. Claire didn't know where Fiji was, and I knew that Rox didn't love her the same way she loved me. I was actually happy to be with both of them.

The lineup moved silently as a shark, making sure its prey did not realize it was in danger until it was too late. Rox dropped herself between Mary Jo and Suzie's towels. Although she startled them, they both seemed to enjoy the attention. It was Rox, after all.

"Dare you to jump in." Rox perked up and ran toward the water.

Mary Jo and Suzie followed, laughing. No one refused a dare from Rox. The beach was empty. No waves, no guys. They knew it was safe to goof around, so they did. Mary Jo and Suzie plowed into the water, hit the ditch, and fell face first into the brown water. Rox, on the other hand, stopped at the shoreline. She did this without either one of them knowing until they came up for air. They booed her, but she just raised her hands into a super-sexy gesture like she was saying "Oh well," and then walked back to her towel.

There's no way to explain the beauty of revenge. Except to say what happened next was worth every speck of Blue Cheer I drank. Neither girl saw what was coming until they returned to the lineup and saw that the Lisas had put their towels about ten feet back from ours.

"Why'd you move our towels?" Suzie asked.

Clearly they were no longer in the lineup.

"What did we do?" Mary Jo whined.

Suzie wasn't going to give in as easily. The towel rearrangement was more than a minor setback for her and she knew it. It was the end.

"You're choosing her over us?" Suzie yelled, pointing at me.

There were no guys around, so everything could hit the fan, and nobody would know. It was girl power to the max. But Rox wanted them shut out without a scene. She lay down on her towel and flipped over to her stomach, ignoring Suzie altogether. Claire, on the other hand, stayed on her feet and put her arm around Mary Jo tenderly.

"You've got to be kidding," Mary Jo said. She was trying to look tough, but her fingers were shaking, and she spit when she spoke. Claire handed Mary Jo the cup of hot coffee and took the lid off.

"I put some cream and sugar in it, just the way you wanted it."

Jenni handed Suzie her cup of coffee and took the lid off as well. She waited for Suzie to drink it, but she just stood there, staring at it.

"Taste it," Jenni said. "Don't you trust me?" Her voice sounded flat and gritty and her tone was hard-core.

"Really. I'm your best friend. Drink it." But when Jenni said "drink it" this time, Suzie stepped away.

I stood shoulder to shoulder with Claire, waiting for Suzie to do something.

"Drink it," Rox repeated without lifting her head.

But Suzie didn't move. She just held the Styrofoam cup in her hand and stared at us.

"It could've been me," Jenni hiccupped.

"No, it couldn't have been." Suzie ripped into Jenni. "What do you think I am, stupid?"

"Yeah, I do. I think you're stupid." And with that, Jenni turned around, lay down on her towel, and closed her eyes.

Suzie threw the cup on the sand. Hot coffee splashed all over Rox and Jenni.

"You bitch," Rox snapped. Her voice carried all the way to the volleyball courts, and a few old guys turned our way.

Suzie looked at the ocean then frantically looked back at Rox yelling, "Watch out, there's a bee!"

Rox threw herself under her towel, sand flew everywhere, and Suzie walked away.

Mary Jo rushed to Rox's side, holding her cup of coffee. She knelt next to her, brushing off the sand.

"I'll drink mine," she said. But before she could, Rox slapped it out of her hands.

"You'll never get Nani's spot, ever."

Rox signaled for all of us to lie down and we did. I closed my eyes as she initiated the silent treatment. Mary Jo paced around us, but stopped directly in front of me, blocking the sun. She stood there for a long time, waiting to see if I'd open my eyes. I told myself: stay tough, cream puff. Finally she walked away. I felt bad but relieved and determined to never back down in front of the lineup. I knew this would secure my spot forever.

☀

When I woke up, KC was looking at me eye to eye. We were shoulder to shoulder on our bellies. I pulled my head back slowly to focus. She smelled like a mixture of Old Spice cologne and Irish Spring soap, like a squeaky-clean guy, not some girl with long eyelashes, perfect skin, and bowed lips. There was not a hint of emotion on her face. She was all tough and cool, as usual.

"Did you have a nice sleep?" Her voice was so soft it was hard to hear. I nodded. We were alone. The rest of the lineup must have gone up for a pee. It was difficult to lift my head. Every part of my body hurt. I did my best to look around casually, like no big deal.

"Don't worry, they'll be back," she said, turning onto her side. Her thumb was tucked under her bikini. She rested her head in her other hand, crossed her long legs, and touched my foot with her foot like we were best friends or something.

She asked, "Do you like Fiji?"

"I don't know what you're talking about," I said. I felt hungover but not so out of it that I would tell her about Rox. Anyway, how did she know about Fiji?

"So you like it," she smiled, and flicked sand in my face.

I sat up with supersonic speed and rubbed my eyes. "What's your problem?"

KC sat up, too. She adjusted her mustard bikini bottom to match her tan lines, then fluffed her shag.

"What are you up to, KC?" Rox asked as she plunked onto her towel and handed me an icy Tab.

"Fiji," was all KC had to say.

"Shut up," Rox commanded.

"Your new chick isn't talking, but I know," KC said.

"We're out of here." Rox motioned me to follow.

I should've kicked sand in KC's face for payback, but when I got up, the world started spinning. I heard KC say, "That Killer's gonna mess you up good, just like she did me. She's gonna dump you for Jerry, and you'll never go to Fiji again."

But Rox had told me she was done with Jerry. KC didn't know anything.

"You're whacked," I told her and walked away.

KC grabbed my ankle. Her grip was strong. It startled me.

"The only person she cares about is Jerry. You are totally screwed."

"Come on, Nani," Rox yelled from halfway up the beach.

"You must be high," I told KC and pulled away so fast I almost tripped and fell face first. I stormed up the beach, trying to catch up with Rox. When I did, she put her arm inside mine and we walked hip to hip onto the volleyball courts. The lineup was waiting. I knew I was different. Whatever happened to that loser KC would never happen to me.

CHAPTER THIRTY-FIVE

Ladies of Leisure

The next morning, I sat at the kitchen table, ready to go to State with Annie's rabbit foot tethered to my belt loop, a thick joint for Lord Ricky, and a purse full of Dad. My horoscope said it was a good day to have a new experience. Finally, I could walk onto the hottest beach in California as a local. I put on a matching bathing suit for the first time. Annie Iopa wore it every year to the Duke Kahanamoku Surfing Championship. The bikini was made of tiny puka shells and jute embroidery. The straps were braided black leather and the fabric was shades of green that matched my eyes. Best of all, it was the smallest bathing suit in the world. Even in Brazil, it would have been considered daring. It felt rough and uncomfortable but it was worth it. State had never seen a suit like this before, and even though I hated Annie, I wasn't about to throw away a fashion statement like this.

Annie had told me to wear it once I made local girl status. Even though she was off my list, I knew once upon a time she would have mailed me a medal or something. After all, I was a ruler in training, second in line to Rox and a full-on dominator. Nothing, absolutely nothing, could stop me from fulfilling my destiny now.

Jean sat opposite me, her forehead resting in her hand. In her other hand she was holding an empty bottle of beer. There were thin slices of cantaloupe on a plate in front of her. The *LA Times* was on her lap and the kitchen still smelled like fish.

"Eagleton withdrew his candidacy for vice president," she said.

As if I gave a flying you-know-what about George McGovern or his mental sidekick. All I wanted was a smooth send-off for Dad. I made a little small talk. I knew that was the key to getting out of there as quickly as possible.

"So, Nixon is totally in again?" I asked.

Jean nodded and gave me an unconvincing smile as she pulled an official-looking envelope from her muumuu pocket. There were two things in it, and she took them out and set them on the table for me to see. One was a deed of sale and the other was a check signed by Michael Kei and made out to her for twenty thousand dollars. Then she went back to the morning news as if they weren't there.

"They say Nixon's staff might be connected to Watergate. I'd like to see them prove that," she said.

I grabbed the check and waved it in her puffy old face. "Wasn't this supposed to be a hundred thousand?" I asked.

"Taxes, Mike said."

That was such BS and Jean knew it. She got screwed.

"Can we live on this forever?" I asked. "Can we still be ladies of leisure? That's what you said we'd be."

Jean didn't answer. Her eyes were swollen, and there were little beads of sweat on her upper lip. She squinted at me and shook her head no. I knew for sure we would never go home again, not even for a trip to the Kahala Hilton. At that moment, it was as if Hawaii vanished off the face of the Earth.

You know how it is when you want to cry but don't? Your lower lip sort of quivers and your eyes water up but don't leak? You have to think of something else super-fast or else it's waterworks a go-go. I imagined a VACANT sign flashing over Jean's head in big red neon letters like an abandoned building on Hotel Street. Just to remind myself once and for all no one was home. There was no Mom. I had to get that through my thick skull. Expecting anything from Jean was stupid and I have never been a stupid person. Supernova Virgos like me don't get thrown. I was never going to be like Jean. Besides, I had someplace to be. I had friends now and Rox. I was never going to be alone like Eleanor Rigby. Jean could go sleep off her morning buzz next to a box full of sand.

"I never should have trusted a Hawaiian," she said, taking the curlers out of her hair and putting the check back in her pocket. "Hawaiians only do right by Hawaiians. I'm just the *haole* widow."

Then she looked directly at me, squeezing the little cross around her neck.

"No more Hawaiians for us. We're done with those people."

I read once if you hold your breath and count to ten slowly, it stops the anger. Since I was about to rip 33 Sage apart, I gave it a try and sucked in hard. I held down the air, trying to reason with myself. Dad was gone. Really gone. And everything he loved was gone, too. I let out the air.

I stood up, carefully putting my purse over my shoulder and taking one of Jean's cigarettes out of the Benson & Hedges box on the table. She peered up and watched me with a puzzled look. I tapped the cigarette a couple times in my palm then pulled some matches out of my purse and lit up right in her face. Her brand tasted like dirt, but to show off my smoking skills I cracked a couple perfect rings right into her cantaloupe. Jean seemed not to notice. She put her cigarette out in her beer.

"They say smoking causes cancer in rats," she said.

"Good thing I'm not a rat," I said, pushing the screen open with my foot and letting it slam behind me. Going down the front path, I stomped on Jean's soft-leafed succulents, smashing them with my heels and watching their innards squish out. I dropped my cigarette on the sidewalk and watched it burn while I tied up my shirt and rolled down my shorts. I brushed my hair hard fifty times. *Five-O*, I laughed to myself.

Don McLean's voice blasted out of the windows above. Maybe Jean would find the secret "American Pie" message today but I seriously doubted it. Nothing could save her. No pop star or God. She was a lost cause. I swore to myself that I'd never depend on her again. She had become a memory even though she was still alive.

The sun was intense. It was the end of August and finally felt like summer. I had an hour before the lineup expected me. There was only one more thing to do before I claimed my permanent spot at State. The sooner I got it taken care of, the better off I'd be.

CHAPTER THIRTY-SIX

※

Funny Kine Honey Girl

This was it.

Channel Lane was a secret street. More of a low bridge, really, that went over the aqueduct leading to State. I ducked down it, checking over my shoulder as I went. The plan was simple: sneak through the creek, zip up to the Jetty, and let Dad go on turtle turf, make it back without anyone seeing me, and cruise onto State. The Jetty, my first beach, would be Dad's *puuhonua*. I think that's what it was called. It was getting harder and harder to remember the exact translation for Hawaiian words, but I think it meant "sanctuary."

I shuffled through my purse looking for a snack. All I found were a few squares of Bazooka bubble gum with sand-caked wrappers. I stuck all four pieces in my mouth at once. It was like chewing a tennis ball. I sucked down the sugary juice, looking at the glass jar filled with teeny bone fragments and ash, trying to get up my nerve.

No matter what it took, I had to keep my balance and get my mojo under control. I hummed a Kui Lee melody. My voice sounded strange to me. It seemed deeper and older.

It wasn't the way I remembered it from school assemblies or sailing with Dad. Something in me had really changed. It was as though I found the missing piece to a map and finally knew exactly where I was going. When the gum went soft, I knew it was time. Dad had to get to the ocean and I had to get to my permanent spot in the lineup.

My towel was wrapped tight around my waist as I walked into the tall dill weeds, looking for a way under the bridge. I was just stepping around the chain link fence that divided the hillside from the street when I heard a mini bike blasting down Entrada Drive.

There they were. Rox and Jerry, swerving slow and wide down the street. Her hands were hidden under his waistband. They were coming directly toward me. Rox's towel flew open behind her like wings, and Jerry looked like he had just woken up with his dark shades, wild hair, and crumpled navy blue trunks. Rox sat snug against his back, leaning over his shoulder. Obviously they were together again.

Before they got to the bridge, I jumped back and tripped over the roots of a giant eucalyptus tree. I grabbed my purse and huddled low, holding my knees. I watched them get off the bike. They were just a few feet in front of me. Jerry stepped up onto the sidewalk and pulled Rox to him and kissed her. Watching their tongues swish around each other's made me sick. They were practically doing it in front of me. And did Jerry have my necklace on?

I stood up, keeping my head low. Jerry did have my necklace on. The red coral and ivory fit snug around his neck.

I couldn't catch my breath; my stomach sank. I was so crazed, I lost my footing again. I teetered back and forth, but there was no stopping my long slide. I grabbed two big handfuls of ivy that laced the sharp incline but couldn't get my balance. I slid a few more feet down and reached out for another bunch of vines. I tugged too hard, and they snapped out of my hands as I fell under the bridge.

It was only a couple of feet, but my bag strap broke and the glass jar pitched into the air. It plunged into the creek and shattered to pieces on the bank. My whole body went stiff. I wanted to scream but couldn't, so I stuck my hand over my mouth. There was nothing I could do but watch my dad's ashes explode into the air and fly away, sparkling like gold dust into the sky. It was as though there was a funnel or a force in that aqueduct that took him away in a single gust of wind.

"What was that?" Jerry asked. I peered up and saw him looking over the bridge just a few feet above me. He had Rox sandwiched in front of him, cupping her breasts.

"Rats," Rox said, pulling Jerry away. "Let's go to our spot."

After I heard them drive off, I ran to the broken jar. A sound came out of my mouth like a high-pitched hiss. I was crying, "No, no, no." Gasping for air, I threw my towel down and kneeled over the broken glass. I clutched my hair to one side and huddled as close as I could to the half-submerged jar. It was awful. What was left of my dad stuck to the bottom. I took a stick and scraped it out, making sure every muddy bit was released.

The creek was only a few inches deep, but it flowed steadily out to sea. This would have to be my father's *puuhonua*.

"Aloha, Daddy," I said. "Thank you for making me Hawaiian. Sorry about the Jesus stuff. I hope your spirit makes it home to warm water. Amen."

I guess you could call it a prayer.

"Who are you?"

I turned my head quickly and gasped, swallowing the wad of gum. My eyes went wide looking up at Lōlō the bum and his dog towering above me. Lōlō wore an orange crate on his head, a wine cork necklace, and smelled like burnt popcorn or something unearthed after the rain. Armpit stains seeped through his coat, and up close I could see his face was layered with thin red lines the size of veins on a shrimp's spine. I tried to stand, but the dog growled and sat on my long hair. I knew better than to move. The dog's skull was bigger than mine, and his mouth was right beside my face. My flip-flops were squishing into the moss that lined the water's edge. When I talked, I couldn't move.

"I'm just a nice Hawaiian going to the beach."

"I didn't ask what you are. I asked who—who are you?" Lōlō sounded like a professor, not some nut with a crate on his head.

"What do you mean?" I asked.

Lōlō dipped down into my face. He had crusty lips and beer breath. I pulled back slowly.

"Don't you know who you are?" he said with a frown.

Maybe it was a trick question. Regardless, I didn't have time for this BS.

A dragonfly buzzed around the dog, Lōlō, and me. Staying perfectly still was hard. The dog's cone-shaped face was moving closer to mine. Doves cooed and some ducks paddled downstream. This was bogus.

I wasn't going to let a whole summer and lifetime of preparation, and years of growing my hair, go to waste now.

I had to figure a way out of here. This wasn't like some wave I could dodge. And there wasn't anyone who could save me. Not a parent. Not a friend. And not Christ. As a matter-of-fact, at that very moment, I broke up with Jesus. How could a loving god stick me in a mess like this after I'd worked so hard? It wasn't fair.

Fine. I got it. Life isn't fair. Big whoop. But I had a place to go and that was State. So there was no way that ugly dog was going to stop me.

I looked up at Lōlō holding his walking stick and made sure I didn't raise my voice. I bit down and just said it, "You wanna know who I am? I'm a *Funny Kine*. I do it with girls and boys."

"Oh, everybody around here does that." Lōlō added a lisp to his words and swayed to one side, holding one hand on his hip and dangling the other limp at the wrist, doing a stereotypical imitation of a gay guy.

I could feel the dog's warm saliva dripping down my shoulder and his tail wagging through my hair.

Lōlō adjusted his crate as if it was a hat and said, "I just want to know your name."

He dipped his head back and forth from one side to the other like a bobblehead hula girl. He unscrewed the cap off a bottle of Blue Nun and took a gulp of wine.

"Nani," I said. "My name is Nani."

"Well Bonnie, who does it with girls and boys . . ."

A cold fear gripped me. I was glued in place, trapped between Lōlō and his dog. Lōlō pointed at the rabbit foot hanging from my belt loop and said to the dog, "Wanna play?"

The dog's thick body hunkered low to the ground, and his tail started wagging faster. His beady black eyes fixed on me, and his paws, the size of my hands, reached out in front of him. Lōlō pointed at the rabbit foot again.

"Toss it, Bonnie," he told me.

Without a second thought, I threw my good luck charm down the canal and ran in the opposite direction as fast as I could. The dog took off; the ducks scattered, and I scrambled up the hill, clutching my bag, telling myself not to stop running until I got to State. I didn't know I could climb so fast or jump a fence. Entrada had a downward slant, and the sidewalks were uneven. I just told myself, *Do not stop running*. Regardless of what I looked like, I had to get safe. That was a new rule:

Safety before beauty.

I didn't think anything could hurt more about Dad, but I totally blew it. I left his ashes in a swamp with a crazy old man and his carnivorous, fang-toothed dog. With a prayer he'd get to warm waters. I gathered my nerves to go into the tunnel alone. Echoes pitched from below mixed with the sound of water dripping and traffic above. I freed my hands, lit up a cigarette, took a deep breath, and charged forward.

CHAPTER THIRTY-SEVEN

Fire with Fire

I heard the mini bike still zipping around the bluffs. I had made it to State before Rox and Jerry. My hair blew off my face, and I lowered my shades, ready for what would come next. Lord Ricky dropped his golf club down like a gate. He adjusted his bathrobe and tipped his cowboy hat back.

"Howdy," he said, extending his hand palm up.

I put the joint in it and waited.

"That is not necessary, ma'am," he said, handing it back to me. He touched Nigel's Saint Christopher with the tip of his metal club. It was cold against my chest.

I took my thumb and pushed the golf club down. Then I leaned in close enough to feel the prickle of Lord Ricky's day-old beard and looked directly into his Ray Bans. The reflection was of a fifteen-year-old woman. Not a girl. I knew how to play by the rules and, better yet, how to rewrite them.

"You can't touch mine, unless I can touch yours." I reached my finger toward his dog tags. Not even his dog tags. The coward wore his best friend's. Lord Ricky gave me a dirty look, and I stopped just before he let loose.

He said, "No way, José."

I removed my finger and told him, "Then don't touch mine."

There were several boards leaning against the stone wall. State was going off. I had to get to the lineup fast. One of the little NP groupies looked up at me like I was a goddess walking on air. Strangely enough, she was playing a string game called "Rock the Cradle." She couldn't take her eyes off of me. This child deserved a note of advice.

She practically bowed to me when I told her to come closer. I cupped her ear and said, "Watch out. Lord Ricky has the clap. You know what that is?" She shook her head no. "Gonorrhea. Be careful." I tore up the joint and tossed it in the trash. I had made it.

᠅

Whatever kind of hysteria I was on the verge of, whether it was laughter or tears, stopped when I saw Claire by the shower, blonde strands blowing across her face. She was back to her normal perfect self, wearing dangling turquoise earrings and her favorite turquoise bikini so low her butt crack showed when she bent over to rinse her foot.

Claire yelled, "Come here. I think I stepped on something."

The shower was on full blast, and water flowed all over her little flat feet. I caught myself thinking, *What a stupid haole. Why doesn't she wear her slippahs?* Then I remembered how bad that sounded when Annie had said it to me. My nerves were rice paper thin. I was only picking on Claire because I felt like such a two-timer. If I could have unzipped my skin and climbed out of it to disappear, I would have, but there was clearly no more running away.

"Do you see glass in my foot?" she asked, placing all of her weight on one leg and lifting her foot so I could examine it. Damn. Even Claire's feet smelt good. I caught whiffs of jasmine mixed with peppermint as I got closer to her heel. There was a stinger or something like it sticking out, just a speck, not in deep.

"I see it," I said and told her to lean on me. I pushed my thumbnails together and squeezed it right out. I had to tell Claire about Shawn before the damsel in distress could shower me with hugs and kisses. I hated myself, hated the way I felt and glanced away quickly so I didn't have to look her in the eye. I just wanted everything to be okay, but telling the truth was a risk I had to take. It would never be right until I told her what happened.

"Claire, I accidently kissed Shawn," I said.

"No you didn't," she said. "Shawn told me what happened."

"Really?" I asked.

Claire wrapped one arm around me and rested the other one on my hip. She said, "Now don't get freaked out, but . . ." she took a deep breath and rattled on. "Nigel pretended to be Shawn, pretending to be him, so he could test your loyalty."

I wanted to say, *do you have bats in your belfry? Are you out of your mind?* But her eyes started to tear up, and she plastered a grin on her face bigger than I'd ever seen. She just looked at me and made sure not one tear fell from her eyes.

"That's what Shawn told me, and that's what I need to believe. Okay, Nani?"

I didn't know what to say, but she looked like she was hanging by a thread or beginning a fall that would never end unless I stopped it. So I took both her hands in mine and looked deeply into her eyes and said, "I'm so relieved it was Nigel. Can we keep this between us?"

That's when I rewrote an important rule:

**Never let a local lose face, especially when she is
your friend.**

"Thanks, Nani," she said, no longer able to keep the tears from falling. She quickly added, "I need to hose off the sand. I'll see you down there." She turned away, dropping her hair, then her face, then her whole body into the cold shower.

"Okay, I'll see you down at the lineup." I don't think she heard me.

It was a Monday, so State was locals only. To the left were a couple happy little gay boys in striped bun-huggers, rainbow Have-A-Nice-Day tank tops with dyed Hershey-brown hair and thin mustaches. Of course they were being hassled, picked on one at a time by some locals telling them to move farther down the beach, that they didn't belong, and what would happen to them if they chose not to listen. Being gay on State Beach was really hard. That would never change no matter how many rules I wrote.

I was closing in on the lineup when someone yelled my name. I looked around, then up.

"Nani," Jerry hollered from the bluffs. Next to him, Rox was waving her arms, crisscrossing them over her head. So that was "their place." How romantic. I clenched my teeth together and curled my lips up into a smile and waved back, muttering, "Up yours."

"Told you so," KC sang out.

Rox pulled Jerry out of sight when she saw KC standing next to me. The mini bike revved up, and I knew they'd be at State pronto. I thought KC would keep walking to the courts, but she was basking in the satisfaction of seeing me dumped. She took a cigarette from behind her ear and a pack of matches from the side of her bikini.

"So?" KC smirked. "Now what are ya gonna do?"

I thought of Pele. I had to fight fire with fire and not turn the other cheek like Jesus. I leaned in ever so slightly. KC's elbow rubbed up against mine.

"It's not the end of the world," I said sarcastically, fluttering my eyelashes. "We still have each other."

"IYD," KC said. In your dreams.

She looked tan and pretty and gazed into my eyes. It was kind of like a typical staring contest or a dare. Neither one of us moved or blinked. We just looked at each other for a long time and didn't smile. I told her, "You're funny."

KC lifted her smoke to her mouth and inhaled deeply before she realized she wasn't lit up. I never stopped staring at her even as she blushed, looking down at her fingertips.

"You dork," I told her, not in a mean way but with a big smile. She wasn't so bad. I took the matches out of her hand so she could see them. Then I lit her cigarette. Fire with fire.

She left her cigarette dangling from her mouth and laughed, shaking her head. She knitted her fingers together and cracked her knuckles loudly.

"You're trouble, Nuuhiwa."

It seemed we had an understanding. I left KC standing in the middle of State and walked toward the lineup.

CHAPTER THIRTY-EIGHT

※

The Middle Ground

"Got ya," Claire said. She snuck up behind me and put her arm through mine just like she did with Rox. She was totally Claire again, all smooth and shiny. We strolled together through a cloud of Nag Champa. The Topangas were smoking clove cigarettes and licking chocolate rolling papers. They had daisy chains in their hair and were trying to make music with their finger cymbals. Did they even know it was 1972 and the sixties were over? I was just about to remind them that Jim Morrison was dead when they said, "Morning, Nani and Claire." I liked the way they chimed my name first.

Jenni and the Lisas lay stretched out on their towels. They lifted their heads and waved with just their fingers. Their bodies were golden-orange and gleamed in the sun thanks to a thick coating of Bain de Soleil. I couldn't believe my eyes when they actually stood up and opened the line for me and Claire to sit in the middle, leaving a small space for Rox. I knew it was respectful to let Claire settle in before I did, so I stood facing the ocean.

The waves were pumping three to five with an offshore breeze. There must have been about twenty guys out. Just as I was tossing my bag into the spot next to Claire, I felt something in the lining. I reached in and pulled out the Band-Aid box holding what was left of Dad. Finding it was like getting a reprieve from the warden at midnight. I was going to get a second chance to put Daddy in the ocean where he belonged.

I clutched my purse and dug my feet deep in the sand. The ocean, waves, sun, and offshore breeze connected me to everything good about my dad, so why was I hesitating? I knew Dad would be more alive in the ocean where things breathed and flowed than if he were stuck in the bottom of my purse or some urn by Jean's bed. My plan was finally going to work. When I swam at State, he'd be with me. All I'd have to do was follow the tide.

"What's wrong, Nani?" Claire asked.

"Oh, the Red Baron struck last night," I joked. What was my problem? I tried to perk up. I had everything under control. There was nothing wrong, I told myself. Letting Dad go was the real natural progression.

Shawn dropped in on Nigel as they both took off on the same wave. Nigel's board flipped out from under his heel, and he fell back. This was my chance. I grabbed the Band-Aid box, tucked it under my armpit, flipped my hair to that side, and ran to the water. As I waded in, churning foam spread around my hips. There was a bit of a riptide, but I was able to stop Nigel's board before it jetted into the ditch and crashed on shore. To the lineup and all the guys in the take-off zone, it looked like I was being the ultimate girlfriend, but really I was being the ultimate daughter. I opened the box and watched my father dissolve into the sea.

"*Aloha mau loa*, Daddy." That meant "I love you forever." No hello. No goodbye.

It's a good thing Nigel was a powerful swimmer. The waves were starting to peak, and the rip was really strong. I could feel it tugging at my legs so hard. I pulled back and let my knees bend slightly to manage the tide, holding Nigel's board steady beside me and keeping my hair from blowing in my face. My beach craft went unnoticed. Rox and Jerry had sauntered to the lineup as Nigel edged closer and closer.

Nigel was my pretty-pretty. What did I want Rox for? What was I thinking? Let Jerry have her. I was lucky to get out of her grip alive. She'd either screw Jerry to death or marry him someday. She'd work full time at the Chart House as a hostess, and Jerry would sell used Fords on Santa Monica Boulevard between surf competitions. They deserved each other. I was going to be like Barbarella and have adventures.

And then again, a rather remarkable idea struck me. Fire with fire. Let Rox get a taste of her own medicine. Nigel caught a tiny wave and body surfed right into me.

"Hey," Nigel said, wrapping his wet body around mine. He nuzzled my neck and bit my earlobe. All the guys in the take-off zone started hooting and yodeling their approval. I knew better than to look at them, but Rox was a different story.

Our eyes met as I turned and said, "Hey," to Nigel. Nigel wasn't even out of breath. I floated his board to him. Now, any other surfer would have gotten his board and split, but

Nigel McBride wasn't just anybody. He took my hand and said, "Thank you."

Who was this guy? I was planning on making Rox jealous, but something else started to happen. The way his eyes sparkled and the corner of his lips slightly curved made me think Nigel McBride was my Honey more than I was his. If it wasn't for him, Rox would have never paid attention to me, and I wouldn't be in the lineup. He was the only person that was 100 percent true blue. I kissed him for real, without an agenda or rule. Not to get something or be someone. I just really liked him. Maybe that was better than love.

It felt like I had my priorities straight even if deep down I wasn't. I think truly the only thing straight about me was my hair. That's when I got it. Rox was a Scorpio, ruled by Pluto and darkness. I was a Virgo, a virgin, ruled by sunlight and ocean. Without someone or something in the middle of us, water and fire could not mix. Jerry and Nigel were the balance between us. The zodiac and our signs completed my understanding of how it was possible to be Rox and Nani, Fiji lovers.

In fact, I finally got it. I wasn't a *haole*. I was Swedish and Irish—and duh, 100 percent American. Jean was a Republican. I wasn't sure what I would be. That was cool. Why couldn't liking girls and boys be like voting? I'd figure out later which side I'd be on.

The trick was finding my middle ground. A personal DMZ. A bridge between rich and poor. Gay and straight. In and out. Jean and Mom. Dead and alive. Hawaiian rules and how to live on the mainland.

Jerry ran into the water. His long hair had highlights in it like mine. His white teeth sparkled and cute little grin teased as he strut into the ocean.

"Better hurry, McBride. Bob's going to call it any second." Rox walked to the lineup. I had that familiar feeling of someone knocking the wind out of me when I saw her. She had her blouse tied low on her hips and her towel draped around her neck like a lei. Her hair swept behind her, making her look airborne and immortal.

Rox adoringly monitored every move Jerry made, especially when he splashed me and powered into the waves. I watched obediently until Nigel caught a wave with total supremacy. He let the curl chase him before he flipped out and somersaulted off his board, showing off. Lisa Y. yelled, "He's so crushed out on you." That was my signal to return to the lineup.

The moment of truth. Where I was placed would determine if Rox was still going to let me rule someday. KC's empty towel was on the far end. Lisa H. came next then Lisa Y. There was an open space for me next to Rox with Claire on her other side and Jenni beside her. From a distance, I could see I was directly in the middle of the lineup. Bull's-eye.

Settling in was not a problem. Not a grain of sand flicked as I laid down my towel, tucked the Band-Aid box into my tote, and stretched out between them.

This was the center of the universe. I had no doubt. The morning smelled of the ocean and the Topangas' assortment of incense. The smell of spicy cinnamon jawbreakers overpowered the suntan oil and cigarette smoke.

I didn't need to smell my father's vodka anymore. But I did have to look at Rox. I couldn't lie next to her and not acknowledge the empress she was. Cautiously, I touched my fingertips to hers.

As the lineup got busy, Rox leaned into my ear and whispered, "This is yours." She fastened my elephant necklace around my neck and clasped it tight. We looked at each other, talking only with our eyes. I wasn't going to take this necklace off ever again, even in the water. It felt good next to Nigel's Saint Christopher.

Rox dropped her voice low into my shoulder. "Jerry and Nigel are for every day," she said. "Fiji is a vacation paradise just for us. Don't forget that." And then, just like that, she sunk low into her towel, checking me out head to toe.

No doubt my sexed out bikini would make her need a psychiatrist by the end of the day. She kept looking at me and then back to the jammed take-off zone, watching Jerry drop in on big waves. I scooped some sand into my hand, making little mounds and flattening them down.

I closed my eyes and went into my dream chamber. It was beautiful again. I imagined myself wearing a fern head lei that looked like a crown of green, watching canoes disappear into the horizon, that place where the ocean and sky merge into a single line. I could almost see my father smiling and hear his warm laughter. That was then and this is now, I told myself, opening my eyes.

Marooned on the mainland or back in Hawaii, all that mattered was this: people would come and go, but a beach would never leave me. The ocean, waves, sun, the offshore breeze, Pele, and the sky connected me to everything good about life and my dad. He was here on my beach at State with me now. I'd always know where to find him, and hopefully he would always know where to find me.